Thumbprint Mysteries

DEAD
BECKONING

BY

ALANNA KNIGHT

D1473029

CB
CONTEMPORARY BOOKS

a division of NTC/CONTEMPORARY PUBLISHING GROUP
Lincolnwood, Illinois USA

Thumbprint
Mysteries

MORE THUMBPRINT MYSTERIES

by Alanna Knight:

The Royal Park Murder
The Monster in the Loch

This is a work of fiction. The characters, incidents, and dialogues are products of the author's imagination and are not to be construed as real. Any resemblance to actual events or persons, living or dead, is entirely coincidental.

Cover Illustration: Gerard Dubois

ISBN: 0-8092-0689-7

Published by Contemporary Books,
a division of NTC/Contemporary Publishing Group, Inc.,
4255 West Touhy Avenue,
Lincolnwood (Chicago), Illinois 60646-1975 U.S.A.
© 1999 Alanna Knight
Manufactured in the United States of America.

90 QB 0 9 8 7 6 5 4 3 2 1

CHAPTER 1

There was nothing to suggest that danger and death lay in wait for me that summer. The events that were to change my life began with a wedding. For most people weddings are important to the happy couple, to families and guests wondering what on earth to buy them and what on earth to wear.

In Edinburgh where I lived with my father above our bookshop in the Royal Mile, business was rather poor as usual. But we now had our own reasons for feeling good about the future.

Surprise, surprise—Dad had asked Susie to marry him! Or so Susie had understood or rather misunderstood Dad's intentions. He looked merely puzzled by all the fuss, and I suspected he might be just a tad deaf to those wedding bells pealing in Susie's ears. It had all come about when Dad broke his ankle and I went off to the Highlands on one of his deals.

Susie had promised to take care of him and the friendship of years had quickly turned into the romance she longed for. Susie's mother who owned the bakery across the road felt that all her prayers had been answered at last, for we both knew that Dad had been Susie's secret passion for years. In my absence Susie moved into our apartment to make it easier to look after Dad and as one thing led to another, she found out that he loved her too. On the strength of this, being Susie, she expected him to want to marry her.

When I returned from the Highlands, even I could see that their relationship had taken on a new dimension, but all my information regarding this spectacular progress came from Susie, not from Dad. He remained silent with a tendency to change the subject when the word *marriage* came up.

One day I asked him direct, "Did you ask Susie to marry you?"

He looked fairly taken aback, but he smiled gallantly and said, "All in good time, my dear."

That was typical of Dad, who was pretty good at ignoring things he didn't wish to discuss. I knew this side of his nature firsthand since he had avoided the topic of my missing mother for as long as I was old enough to ask questions!

"Susie seems to think you proposed and that she accepted," I said firmly.

"Oh, does she now?" Dad's shrug said more than a page full of words. If only Susie could have seen it as he said with a shrewd glance in my direction, "Let's say I'm prepared to give it more careful thought once you and Calum name the day."

So that was his crafty game, I thought. Let Susie blame it all on me.

"To be tactful, Annie. You wouldn't want to share this tiny apartment with another woman. Think of the two of you in a kitchen of this size!"

So Dad had called my bluff. Since I was his daughter and he thought he knew me better than anyone, I guess he had already realized I was taking more time than was necessary in arranging my own wedding to Detective Sergeant Calum Crail, whom I loved dearly.

As far as I was concerned, I could see life with Calum waiting for me like a cozy homecoming. Like a bird winging home to a nest, I would settle down to it one day, but meantime there were important things I had to sort out, riddles that I had to solve first.

And those riddles, although he didn't know it, concerned my father too. Dad led everyone (including his future son-in-law Calum) to believe that my missing mother was dead. But was she? And if so, how had she died, and why wouldn't he talk about it if it was that long ago, for heaven's sake? In fact, I sometimes wondered if that was the real reason why Dad wasn't ready and eager to name his wedding day with Susie.

And that was the main thing I had to find out before I married Calum. Why had Dad always refused to tell me what had happened when I was a child and my mother vanished from our lives?

So while Susie made up guest lists and gazed dreamily into shop windows at wedding dresses, I tried to evade the same subject with Calum. He had decided we were getting married that summer. Instead of guest lists and wedding frocks, he was always dragging me away to look at the latest lists of houses for sale in Edinburgh. We only looked at the ones we could afford—and I didn't fancy living in any of them.

I wanted a house at least a hundred years old, but I

would settle for an apartment in an historic building like the one I had lived in all my life.

"No," said Calum firmly. "A modern house with a nice garden. Let's be practical, Annie. Historic flats are no good for bringing up kids. All those stairs to climb and nowhere to play. We must have a garden for me to grow our own vegetables and a place for Nero (the dog) and kids to play in."

Kids! Wait a minute! I wasn't even prepared for the long walk down the aisle yet. Marriage and wedding bells were one thing, but beyond the altar sounded that cracked bell from the past, the nightmare I was never to escape. Yet my saner moments said that I should marry Calum quickly and let the past go hang. I should pretend that my mother had died a natural death.

But it was no good. Before I tied the knot, I knew I must know for certain sure whether I had been responsible for my mother's death. Especially since I had a piece of evidence, one tiny clue to set me off on my search.

My visit to the Highlands on Dad's behalf had revealed a link to my mother's early life with a village called Stormer. Knowing of its existence was like an itch I couldn't leave alone.

On good days, I told myself to forget the whole thing, saying that if I found out the truth about my mother, not only might it be a disaster for me but it might destroy the future for Dad and Susie. She seemed like his great chance of happiness after a long time alone.

A solitary scholarly man, he was more at home with his books and characters from fiction than real live women. A very private person was Hamish Kelty, and I doubt if he let anyone get to know him, his daughter least of all.

The first event that was to alter the pattern of my life

was a wedding—and not even in my own family circle. Calum's best buddy in the Edinburgh City Police was marrying a girl whose home was in Airdbenn on the west coast, in that desolate edge of Britain where there's nothing between Scotland and America except the Isle of Skye and the great rollers of the vast Atlantic Ocean.

The second event was that Susie had a new craze. Knitting! No big deal, since every other shop in the Royal Mile along from Hamish Kelty's Bookshop sells Aran and Fair Isle sweaters.

Hand knitting is the Scottish tradition, a way of life that goes back centuries to the fisherfolk who knitted into their men's garments the folklore, the superstitions, and the local legends of the seal women, of trolls, and of strange Celtic gods.

Susie hadn't done much knitting since her schooldays until the day Dad remarked at supper that he had always worn hand-knitted socks when he was a lad and what he had always longed for was an Aran sweater like his Highland mother had knitted for him.

For Susie, it was a simple step from socks to sweaters. Even Calum looked wistfully in my direction as Susie was never to be seen any longer without her knitting needles and balls of wool. But I pretended not to notice or hear his deep sigh.

Susie got me aside: "You should learn, Annie Kelty. All those hours sitting behind a counter waiting for customers. Knitting's what I intend to do once I marry your dad. Instead of sitting in a shop doing nothing."

"I read books," I protested.

She ignored that. "You should knit instead—for Calum. It would stop you biting your nails," she added sternly as I thrust them quickly out of sight. "I've watched you when you're reading. You want them to look nice when you get married, and you'd give them a chance to grow. You couldn't bite them like that if you had a pair of knitting needles in your hands and a pattern to follow."

I should point out here and now that when Susie finds a new hobby or some new food that everyone else has known about for years and years, she insists that all the folk around her share her excitement. And so it happened when I was talking about what to wear for the wedding at Airdbenn, she stopped counting stitches, put down the knitting needles, and gave a little scream.

"Airdbenn, did you say? My knitting yarn comes from a place near there. Can't remember its name—but Airdbenn's the nearest town."

"I didn't know that."

(Enter the hand of destiny!)

"You wouldn't since you don't knit. They make this dreamy knitwear in the boutiques on Princes Street. Costs the earth, of course. Their products are pure wool, no synthetics, all made from their own sheep and natural dyes.

"They've only just reached London shops too. You can see models in *Vogue* magazine. They sell yarn too but it's hard to get hold of and it's wildly expensive. The village is only a few miles from where you're going with Calum. You could get me some more because the shop has run out of that dye. I'd love some samples too!" she added, clapping her hands together in great excitement.

"Are you thinking of setting up a knitting industry or something?" I interrupted with difficulty.

"Of course not. But if I had a few samples, then I could buy from them direct, cut out the middleman." She added with a sly glance at Dad, "It would save us money, you know."

By this time, you are wondering what on earth weddings and knittings have to do with my search for my mother. Quite a lot, as it happened, and as I was to find out later when Calum spread his road map of Scotland on the kitchen table to plan our journey to Airdbenn.

As Susie and I looked over his shoulder, she said, "It's there somewhere—"

One word jumped out at me. Seven tiny black letters, hardly visible to the naked eye.

"Stormer! That's the place, Annie."

I hardly listened to Calum's history of the Isle of Skye and its romantic connections with Bonnie Prince Charlie and Flora Macdonald. I could only think of Stormer. I had reason to believe that my mother had been there, and it was just a few miles from Airdbenn.

I made my plans carefully. Of course I was going to Jim's wedding. I love weddings and had been invited anyway as Calum's fiancée. But as soon as I could afterwards, I'd slip away and head for Stormer.

There was only one snag. Calum's mum had Irish relatives who had moved from Belfast to Oban, like Airdbenn on the west coast of Scotland. As it was in easy traveling distance, the chance of a big family party was not to be missed.

How on earth was I going to get out of that one? Being me, I'd think of something.

And so we set off from Edinburgh with Calum looking super in full Highland dress—tartan kilt and sporran, velvet jacket with lace at his wrists and neck, and a dagger tucked into his tartan socks. A real picture.

As always happens when the men wear full Highland dress, the ladies are rather more subdued. I had a pretty cream silk suit and a big cream wedding hat covered in tulle and flowers that was out of this world.

We started off and I realized I had never been this far

west in Scotland before. As Calum drove along the narrow twisting roads beyond the trees and hedgerows, the scenery was breathtaking. Great rocky cliffs, wild seas, and the Atlantic Ocean. There was nothing to equal this scenery on the east coast. The Firth of Forth where I had lived all my life was smooth and dull as glass by comparison.

At my side, Calum was eager to talk weddings, our own in particular. I wasn't saying much. I was rather busy thinking about how I was going to get out of that family party in Oban and go to Stormer on my own.

My chance came almost as if fate were on my side for once.

A Highland wedding is like no other occasion on God's earth. It has to be heard and seen and lived through to be believed! The *ceilidh* (cay-lee), or wild dancing, that followed would last for days. I don't think even Calum was able to cope with all that and the booze.

Poor Calum. He's no great drinker at the best of times. He doesn't like to admit it, but a couple of glasses of wine with a meal is about his limit—and mine.

At Jim and Marie's wedding, thanks to the heavy amounts of *usquebaugh*, or neat whiskey, being gulped down like glasses of mineral water, alas, he got very seriously drunk and passed out.

One of the guests, the local doctor, looked at him lying there and said, "Don't expect much of him for the next twenty-four hours. He's out cold, I'm afraid. And when he wakes up, he'll have one hell of a hangover. Give him some of these. They should help."

He handed me a few pills and I asked, "When will he be fit to travel? We were going on to Oban."

The doctor shook his head. "I'd advise you to do the driving or delay your journey for a while when he's taking the pills. They'll tend to make him drowsy."

There wasn't much point in telling him I didn't drive. But there was no way I was going to cool my heels in a hotel room watching over my sick lover for the next two days.

In two days I could be in Stormer and back again. Up to now I had never told Calum of my plans. This was my chance to creep away quietly while he was sleeping off the booze and without any of the arguments I knew he would produce.

And I could see no reason then why I shouldn't be back from Stormer before he was fit to drive on to Oban. In fact, I could do the journey so fast he'd never know I'd been gone. Or so I thought!

From Calum's address book I got the cousins' Oban number. I called and told a young woman with an Irish accent that Calum had a gastric bug and we'd have to delay our arrival for a day or two.

She was sorry, she said. "But give him my love. Tell him not to worry. He won't miss the party; it's not until the weekend. There'll still be plenty of food and Guinness and Irish whiskey too. You won't miss a thing, really."

I was glad I didn't have to pass that message on to Calum—it would have done nothing for his present state of health. So I quickly wrote a note saying I'd called his family and that meanwhile I was going in search of Susie's knitting wool. I'd call him from Stormer and we could revise our plans. Perhaps I could take a bus and meet him in Oban.

He hardly stirred when I kissed him good-bye. "G'be, love, have g'd time," he groaned and turned his face to the wall. I changed into jeans and tennis shoes, left my wedding finery in the car, and had a quick look at the map. Stormer was only twenty miles away, and I decided that there must be some kind of public transport since

Airdbenn was on the main road. There might even be some wedding guests driving home in that direction.

The girl at the reception was very helpful. "You're in luck. There's a hired minibus that brought some of the guests. It's taking them home again. Let's see—it goes past the road end—here. It's only two or three miles to Stormer. But you'd better look sharp. It's about to leave!"

Two or three miles, I thought. I could easily manage that. I walked that distance in Edinburgh every day. I was rushing down the hotel steps towards the bus when I ran straight into the arms of a young guy also in a great hurry.

He was carrying a fiddle case, and I realized he was one of the band who had been playing at the *ceilidh*. Dark eyes, black hair, and olive skin—Celtic looks that at first glance make you think of sunnier, warmer shores than the British Isles.

He stepped aside, said sorry, and grinned at me. I'd heard the band call him Danny Lucas and I'd been aware of him during the dancing. Our eyes met often as I danced past with Calum and he seemed to be looking directly at me.

I knew all about that chemistry thing. Once when I was sitting out and Calum had left in a hurry to be sick, I saw Danny quickly leave the platform, whisper to his friends, and head toward me. Without being told, I knew he was coming to ask me for a dance! Pleased, I was all ready to accept when Calum's buddy Jim, the blushing bridegroom, cut in and said sternly that this was our dance.

Danny had looked at me with a little shrug and a grin that said: "Better luck next time."

But there wasn't a next time. At least not then.

CHAPTER 2

The bus journey taking the wedding party homewards was almost as much fun as the wedding itself. There was an air of great jollity in which they sang all the popular songs from long ago. In fact, most of the songs, like the folks who were singing them, had been written long before my dad was born. Many were from movie musicals and favorites from the Second World War.

I'd been hoping for Celtic, rousing tunes to lead ancient heroes into battle. Instead it was "I'll see you again . . . We'll meet again . . ." I thought Dad would have liked this a lot, or would he? I had never seen him the worse for drink when his natural shyness might have taken a backseat for a while.

I settled back for a chance to enjoy some of the scenery rushing past the windows. There was plenty of it, great cloudscapes, wild seas, and huge cliffs.

But this delight was not to be. Most of the men and some of the women were still passing the booze from hand to hand. I was almost knocked out by the smell alone, without a drop of it touching my lips. The men flirted with me but it was harmless, good-natured teasing. To them, I was just a wee lass like one of their own children, in need of cheering up—or so they whispered to steely-eyed wives who thought they were going too far.

I guessed they mostly worked farms in the area. I was sure they worked hard and didn't have many occasions for a high old time, so good luck to them. Saying "No" firmly for the umpteenth time to a swig from the next bottle heading my way, I turned to watch the passing scenery. But alas, it had vanished! All the heavy breathing and singing inside the bus had steamed up the windows, and it was now impossible to see anything through them.

No one minded that but me. So I put on my Walkman, closed my eyes, and let some light music take the place of the merriment all around me. I think I even dozed a little, jerked awake by stops on the way—very necessary and very often with all that intake of liquor.

Comforts stations were nonexistent—a rock and a few thin hedges were all that the roadside could offer by way of privacy. But no one cared, least of all the women. The men who were better equipped by Mother Nature for such bodily functions roared with laughter. Their coarse jests set the women screeching with mirth.

There were few inhibitions left for this little group as the bus shed its passengers at the end of lanes that led to farms hidden from the road. The driver would have taken them to their front doors had it been possible, but the idea of having to turn the bus and get back onto the road or getting stuck in a ditch was beyond his good nature.

"Aye, Jock. The walk in all that fresh air will sober ye up, nae doubt," was his usual response to the grumblers. We cheered on their unsteady steps up the farm road until the next bend in the road hid them from view.

"Hey—you, lass!"

All heads turned round, smiling at me.

"This is your stop for Stormer, lass."

I wiped away a little circle from the steamy window. What I saw outside didn't cheer me very much. And it was even worse when I got outside. Even the cheery shouts of good luck didn't help the bleak scene before me.

I panicked, standing there seeing the bus drive off down the road. I wished with all my heart that I had stayed in my seat, safe and warm to wherever the bus might be going.

I put down my backpack, thankful at least that I had so little to carry.

My choice of luggage had not pleased Calum. He was in favor of traveling to a wedding with the smartest possible suitcases. "You won't need that old backpack this time, Annie."

"Why not?" Going on to Stormer was only an idea then, and it was difficult in Edinburgh to tell him that I fancied a side trip on my own. I knew all about Calum's smart luggage, and I didn't want to be left carrying a case that weighed a ton even when it was empty.

"Why not?" he repeated. "Well, a backpack isn't very smart, is it? I mean, it would hardly make a good impression at a luxury hotel!"

That was true. Mine was shabby and old and covered in labels. But I loved it.

Although I didn't talk back, he saw by my face that I was hurt. Kissing me, he said, "I don't mind, honey, but it does make you look like a teenage hippie. A hitchhiker."

I grinned. "That's all right by me."

It was his turn to look unhappy. I knew what was in his mind. He wanted to be proud of me, to show me off as the right sort of wife for a detective sergeant who was going places in the Edinburgh City Police.

Perhaps he knew even then that the Annie Kelty of today was not quite the same girl he had courted as Officer Crail on his daily beat down the Royal Mile. But was he the same cop who had fallen in love with the girl he saw through the window of Hamish Kelty's bookshop?

I felt suddenly sad that I was letting him down. I think he had guessed by now that I didn't care a lot about climbing social ladders with him and that I might never want to do so. That wasn't easy to explain to an ambitious young cop like Calum. It was hard to accept that the "you" he fell in love with was already shaped before he met you, fixed in stone and likely to remain so.

I still loved him and I believed that I always would. He was ace, the very best, but I had to have space, a life of my own that was more than just making a home and babies. The problem was that I was hungry for more of the same thrills and excitement I had lived through twice during the past year. The world of crime had come to my own front door when my father was accused of murder. Against all the odds, I had set out to find the real killer and had saved Dad from prison.

I had set foot in the criminal world a second time by taking a valuable and historic goblet to a castle in the Highlands when Dad broke his ankle. There once again, I had managed to outwit two villains and bring them to justice.

I had to admit that both times some credit went to Calum. If he hadn't arrived on the scene in the nick of time, the story of Annie Kelty would have had a very nasty ending. I would always be grateful to him for saving my life. But two narrow escapes from death still weren't enough, it seemed. I had to go on. I had one more mission—to solve the mystery of my mother and why she had disappeared from my life!

Perhaps my hands were already bloodied. In those dark hours before the dawn, I sometimes awoke from bad dreams, having *almost* remembered the past and what had happened. Was I responsible for her death? Was that the real reason my father refused to talk to me about her?

Such were my thoughts that day as I stood on top of a hilly road with a cold wind blowing in my face. Below me it was as if a gray curtain had swept aside to reveal a different world from the one I had imagined through the bus's steamed-up windows.

I had forgotten there would be no trees. At least none worthy of comment in this land of rocky shores and wild seas.

Unlike Edinburgh's parks with their great trees and leafy branches whispering far above my head, trees in this part of Scotland had a hard life, growing close to the walls of the farms for dear life, as if they needed all the help they could get to stay alive.

And yet—I sniffed the air. There was the smell of peat from distant fires, not from Stormer itself but from unseen farms beyond the barren rocks. The smell was great, very comforting and bringing in its wake hopeful thoughts of farm teas with hot scones.

I breathed deeply. Beyond that fragrant peat smoke a few clouds floated lazily by in a bright blue sky. Soft and plump as angels' pillows, they made a strange contrast to this stern wild land far below them.

Susie would have loved it! I felt suddenly homesick,

wishing she were here to share this moment with me. Ahead a crazy road twisted, down and down, through craggy rocks towards a tiny group of gray-roofed houses huddled together on the very edge of the Atlantic Ocean.

The signpost "3 miles" did little to cheer me. Hopes of a lift down to Stormer faded since only the sturdiest cars would ever tackle it.

I thought about Laverock Knitwear. Considering the road that was little more than a farm track, any folks with craft shops were very brave and lucky to have found their way into Edinburgh shops. I felt sure it would take more than some very expensive hand-knitted sweaters and some lively colored yarns to establish this outlandish spot on the map as a thriving home industry.

Glad to have shed my designer wedding finery for my jeans again, I took up my backpack and set off down the hill. I kept well to the middle of the road, which was kinder to the feet than the stony edges.

And as I walked, my footsteps were echoed by the boom of the sea, the drum of the breakers beating against the shore, and the hoarse cries of seabirds flying above the tiny harbor. From the hillsides above the craggy rocks came the mournful bleating of sheep. The bleak scene was broken now and then by a croft or small farm perched on some grassy outcrop, a lonely sight with windows and doors turned inland away from the bitter sea winds.

The road stretched empty in both directions, so I put on my Walkman and began to sing. This always cheered me up although my singing silenced all those near to me. They handled their distress bravely and with great tact, usually by gently asking, "Would you like a cup of tea perhaps?"

Suddenly I was aware of another sound. The road

shook under my feet, close at hand. A second later, brakes screeched at my heels.

I turned sharply and sprang aside, too late to avert the disaster. There was a skidding sound and the phut-phut of an engine that squealed into silence. I was in time to catch sight of a motorcycle as it whirled out of sight over the edge of the road.

This was followed by a loud bang. I followed the sound. Peering over the rocks, heart hammering, I expected the worst. Instead I saw the motorcycle lying on its side, wheels whirring against a bank of heather. Beside it a tall man clad in black leather looked dazed and shaken. And very cross.

I ran toward him. "Are you hurt?"

"No. Just damn mad. Look at my bike. What the hell were you doing walking down the middle of the road?"

"I thought the road was empty—I'm sorry—"

"You'd just turned a sharp bend. Didn't you notice that?"

"I didn't hear you." I avoided looking at the bike. "I'm sorry," I repeated.

"You must be stone deaf." Then he looked at me for the first time and saw the Walkman round my neck.

"Oh, so it's you. I might have know we'd meet again somewhere."

When he took off the helmet, I saw it was Danny Lucas, the fiddler from the band who had played at the wedding. He ran a hand through black Indian-straight hair and shook his head. He looked over the bike and grinned at me.

"Is the bike all right?" I said anxiously.

"Sure. Takes more than a little leap in the air to worry this little beauty. What about you? What are you doing in this remote part of the world?"

I pointed to the village. "That's where I'm heading."

He was rubbing his ankle.

"Look," I said, "I'm dreadfully sorry. You could have been badly hurt. It just never occurred to me—I thought I was in a deserted world."

"And there aren't many of those anymore, Annie."

Annie! "You know my name!"

"Sure I do. I heard it plenty at the *ceilidh*. Except for the bride, you were the belle of the ball," he added with an admiring glance, a glance that said it wasn't just the designer cream suit that had drawn his attention. "In fact, you may not have realized, but I was coming to ask you for a dance."

"And Jim cut in."

"Yeah! And who could resist the blushing bridegroom!"

We both stopped, looked at each other, and burst out laughing.

"Going to Stormer, are you?" he said.

"Yes."

"All alone?" He raised an eyebrow.

"Yes."

"Ditched the man in your life, have you?"

"Only temporarily. He has family to see in Oban. We're meeting there later. I wanted to see Stormer."

I didn't know why I was making all these excuses. What business was it of his where I went?

"Not much to see down there."

"Why are you going, then?"

"Necessity. I have to work for a living, not like some. I play with a band when I'm not working as a hotel chef."

"And you find plenty to keep you occupied."

I sounded surprised and he smiled again. It was a very nice smile. Very nice lips and white teeth. He was so good-looking I wondered why he'd never tried television.

"Not so much now, but plenty in the tourist season." He glanced at the bike again, jumped on, and tried the engine. It started.

He gave a sigh of relief, looked at me, and said, "That's all right, then. So what are we doing standing here talking? I could be taking you down to Stormer. Hop on, if you don't mind riding on back."

"I'd be delighted."

"OK." And diving into the carrier, he pulled out a helmet. "Behold—I always carry a spare. Never know when it might come in useful. Like now," he said, fastening it on my head and adjusting the strap. "Off we go. Comfortable?"

I was. Very. With my arms around his waist—flying through the air. What an adventure! What a beginning!

But never a thought to how it was all to end. Or to what awaited me in Stormer.

CHAPTER 3

My arms tightly around Danny's waist, crouched behind him on the motorcycle didn't give me much chance to enjoy the scenery. The road had turned into a very bumpy track strewn with boulders. Marks made by thick tires hinted that it was now mostly used by farm tractors.

I decided that Stormer wasn't the place to arrive at or leave in a hurry. Tourists and visitors must bear in mind that time and patience were a necessary part of their luggage. Breathtaking scenery only came into its own once the track smoothed out again into a paved road. It led downwards into a cluster of gray houses with a long twisting street and a harbor wall holding the sea at bay.

On the grassy hillside behind the village, roofless crofts told a tale of better days now lost forever. The walls of an ancient church, with a graveyard whose army of tombstones leaning this way and that, hinted that there might be more dead folk than live ones in Stormer that afternoon.

It was obvious that the sea ruled here in Stormer. You didn't go down to the sea—the sea came up to meet you. It was just yards away from where we stood, great foaming waves beating against a rocky shore that seemed to tremble under the weight of the breakers.

You felt the sea was having a good look at you and considering whether you were worth swallowing up. A big, predatory sea and very scary, I thought and decided then and there to keep a careful distance between us at all times.

But beyond this monstrous sea that held center stage, there were islands visible. Like the humps of beached whales, they stretched toward the horizon. Those nearest Stormer seemed at first glance empty of all life, until the gray rocks moved and turned into grazing sheep.

I looked toward the headland and there perched high above that roaring sea, a tall and once lovely mansion was etched against the sky. The views must have been superb from the great windows staring toward the horizon.

I was puzzled. Who would live there? What sort of people would build a house in such a lonely, dangerous place, exposed to the four winds? Looking more closely now, I saw iron gates and high walls. The house was deserted, the windows without glass, the walls without a roof.

"Here we are," said Danny as the motorcycle engine faded. He handed me my backpack. We had come to the parting of the ways.

He saw me staring at the ruined mansion. "When did that happen?" I asked.

Danny shrugged. "Stormer Hall has quite a history, I believe. The family died off, no heirs, usual sort of thing." He didn't sound very interested.

"Is it very old?"

"Not as old as it looks. Built by a wealthy whiskey millionaire at the beginning of this century. He decided to set himself up as the local laird so he built two roads. A private one leading up to the Oban road where you left the bus." He tapped his foot on the ground. "And this one down to the village. This track is all that's left of it now. No money to keep it in good repair."

"How did he lose all his money?"

"He was smuggling his whiskey across to the States during Prohibition. Thought he had a great deal going. Unfortunately, the gang lords over there forgot to pay him. He went bust and shot himself. His son inherited what was left, but he lost out during the Second World War. His grandsons were killed and the place has never been lived in since."

I felt suddenly chilly, standing there no longer protected from the sea wind by Danny's broad leather-clad back. Chilly and uneasy. Something stirred in my heart at that moment and said in words loud and clear, *You should never have come here. You should have left well alone. You should have stayed with Calum, stayed where you were safe!*

These words were to be repeated over and over. This was just the curtain-raiser.

I watched Danny propping up the bike by the churchyard and covering it with a large green waterproof sheet.

"Will it be safe enough left there?" I asked.

He laughed at my doubtful expression. "I don't think there'll be many takers from over the wall there, do you?

As I handed him my helmet, he stored both of them in the carrier on the cycle. "Well, this is where I leave you. See your way ahead. You can't get lost."

I stared at him. He saw the uncertainty in my face and said, "Where do your friends live?" He waved a hand toward the cluster of houses. "As you see, there isn't much to Stormer. All there is you can see."

"Is there a guest house?"

"A guest house?" he repeated and shook his head. "I thought you had friends here." His amused look said what he thought of anyone coming to Stormer who hadn't friends or connections.

"This is just a fleeting visit," I said, "to see the Laverock factory. They sell their knitwear in Edinburgh."

He shook his head and stared at me as if I had gone mad. "It's at the end of the village. Great barn of a place." With a grin he asked, "Isn't this rather a long way to come to buy a woolly jumper? You'd have saved time and effort by writing for a catalog."

"I wanted to buy some yarn."

That was beyond him. He sighed and ran a hand through thick hair, long and glossy as a raven's wing. Here was a madwoman, all right. I could read his thoughts. He was wondering what he had let himself in for by giving me a lift down the hill.

"That wasn't my only reason," I told him. "Some of my family lived here—long ago. I felt I had to see the place—my roots—"

Danny just watched me and then as I stopped for breath, he smiled gently as if he understood completely.

I hoped the smile wasn't meant to humor me and that he didn't really think I was crazy.

An interesting thought occurred to me. "Where do you stay?" I asked.

He pointed across to a slope where the rocks smoothed out into a grassy slope. "Up there. I have a living van."

"This hotel where you work. Why don't you stay there?"

He shook his head. "It's residents only, I'm afraid. No boarders." He was silent for a moment, watching me as if he were trying to read my thoughts.

"So what are we going to do with you? The nearest town is twenty miles away—back where you came from. Don't get me wrong. I don't want to sound like a heel, but I'm not exactly feeling like going there and back again—"

"I wouldn't dream of letting you do such a thing," I said hotly.

The wind from the sea was getting stronger. We were having to shout a bit.

"That's a relief! So come on," he said and took my arm, leading me up the grassy path.

"Where are we going?" I asked as if I didn't know.

"To the van. We'll have a coffee and think of something."

The van was quite large—the kind I suspect that film stars use on location.

He opened the door. "There's all the usual conveniences in there. I'll put the kettle on."

The tiny bathroom was cute. Catching sight of my wild-looking face in the mirror, I was glad of a chance to use soap and water and apply a brush to my tangled hair.

When I came out, Danny was thrusting papers into a drawer like one making a desperate move to tidy up the place, but when he turned toward me suddenly, he looked startled. I realized that somehow I had caught him off guard. He wasn't expecting me back so soon and he had a distinct air of guilt, something he didn't want me to see.

The table was set by the window which formed one end of the van. Gratefully, I drank the coffee which was very good and admired the view right down across the village and beyond to the islands. I admired the van's interior, the padded window seats, the neat tables, and the way every space was cleverly used. Tables and benches, even a bed was made to fold back into the wall.

I also noticed there were no pictures on the walls, but there were patches with tape and traces of Blu tack— just the right size to suggest that photos had been hastily removed. So as we talked of this and that, I studied Danny a little more carefully.

Obviously he hadn't wanted me to see this room before he had a chance to remove the photographs.

Why? I was a complete stranger to him. So what was it he didn't want me to see? Had it some connection with that guilty pushing things out of sight while I was in the bathroom?

A moment later I thought I had the connection.

"I could offer you a corner of the van," he was saying. And that, of course, was the answer to the mystery. Quite simple.

Girls! Danny had a steady girlfriend, maybe more than one. Or perhaps he liked erotic photographs and thought I would be offended. I looked again. The patches on the wall were standard photo prints rather than posters.

Well, well. I considered Danny again and guessing what was going on in his mind about this girl he'd picked up, I was flattered that he thought I was worth a try.

"It's a good offer. How do you feel about it?" he asked quietly so as not to scare me off.

"Oh, no. I couldn't possibly," I said too harshly and blushed because his mocking glance said that his offer had shocked me.

"No panic, Annie. I was only teasing." With a shrug he turned his back on me and poured out more coffee. Did I detect that he was a tad disappointed when he said, "There is one place where you might get a room for the night. Look, you can see it from here."

He moved over so I could look down on the village. "That old house near the ruined church. It was the manse once. There's a nice old bird, retired schoolmistress, bit eccentric but kind. A middle-aged daughter lives with her—delicate or something—she's lame, walks with a stick. Don't think they have much in the way of money, so they might be grateful."

He paused and looked at me to see how I was taking it. "I'd give you a good reference."

"On such short acquaintance? Would that persuade them to take in a stranger?"

"Well, let's put it this way. They like me," he said with a disarming smile. "I do odd jobs for them. Fix shelves and so forth. When they need a man's help, send for Danny."

I looked down on the grim old manse with its high walls.

From this distance, it looked like a grim old face. Windows like tiny eyes stared across to the sea. The tall narrow door was unwelcoming. I felt suddenly scared again. I'd seen a house like that in my dreams. "What about the hotel? Couldn't you put in your good word for me there?"

Danny shook his head. "All they do is provide meals for the fishermen who come in from the bay and the occasional tourists brave enough, or lost enough, to venture down from the top road. Or hitchhikers, but their prices are a bit steep for casuals. In fact, they don't encourage the pub-lunch kind of trade."

"And you do the cooking for them?"

"Some of it. I am a trained chef. Worked in London before I came here."

I was dying to ask what on earth had brought him to Stormer, but there was something in the way Danny stood up and gathered the mugs and swilled them in the sink that ended the talk between us.

A batty old woman with an invalid daughter didn't sound great to me, but I said, "OK. The manse it is."

He seemed relieved and as he dried his hands, I looked at the bookshelf. He had a taste for thrillers, a few American and British names I knew, but a lot more were in Spanish or Italian.

"Ready then?"

"You are clever," I said.

"How so?"

I indicated the books. "Takes me all my time to read them in English."

He shrugged. "Good practice for traveling."

I could have thought of easier ways and means of getting to know a language. But then languages weren't my thing at all.

Danny didn't say any more. His face had a closed-in look. Or was he just bored and fed up since I hadn't taken up his offer of sharing the van and whatever else that implied?

I chuckled to myself. Wait until I tell Calum about this one! Then sense prevailed. I was going to have enough trouble explaining why I had deserted him, leaving him all alone with a first-class hangover right after the wedding to go off on a jaunt on my own.

I guessed poor Calum would be feeling bruised. It would be wise to make very light of my meeting with the drop-dead gorgeous Danny.

But as we walked down the hill back to the village, I knew I wanted to know more about Danny. He was about my age, perhaps even younger, too old to be a student. He was obviously well-educated—he read thrillers in foreign languages, for heaven's sake!

He was talking about the village. "The church has been a ruin for years. But there has always been a religious settlement here since the day when St. Brida paid the island a brief visit in a storm. When she was shipwrecked, she built a shrine as a thank-you note.

"However, there hasn't been a minister living in the manse since the First World War after the church's roof fell in—a big storm swept the islands. There was never enough money to pay for another. And the people gradually disappeared when the herring fishery folded."

When he paused for breath, I said, "I noticed all the ruined crofts on the way down."

"That's Stormer's story, Annie. Like a lot of other places you'll find up and down the coast. There's a retired doctor who lives here, nice old guy, not much needed. People here are pretty healthy. As for their souls, well, the parish minister holds a service every second Sunday in the social hall. He does the boat trip, island to island—"

As I listened I wondered what Danny's secret life was all about. He didn't look like a dropout. There was something purposeful about him. So why was he wandering around Scotland, playing the fiddle (which, I remembered from that wedding *ceilidh*, he did uncommonly well) and doing shifts as a chef in an out-of-the-way hotel and odd jobs for a couple of old ladies?

I decided this was one mystery that would have to remain unsolved. I had a priority which I must keep firmly in mind. And that was to find out about my mother and get back to the hotel and Calum as soon as possible.

And time wasn't on my side. Danny would remain one of those chance encounters, the kind I had always dreamed about. The hero of romances and films that women have fantasies about meeting.

If only I had left then. If only it hadn't been Danny I met but some dull family in a car who had taken the wrong turn and given me a lift to Stormer.

If only I had gone back to the shore road and left the mystery of Danny alone. If only I had left the older mystery of my mother where it belonged, buried in the past.

CHAPTER 4

As soon as I set foot on the path to the manse, I knew I had taken the wrong turning. Too late to go back now, but the air twitching my nostrils had that familiar tang of danger close at hand.

Danny tapped on the door and called, "Hello there?" Without waiting for a reply, he walked swiftly along a short corridor. It was stacked with bookshelves. An encouraging sight—I would never lack something to read during my short stay.

He tapped on a door and shouted, "It's Danny, Mrs. MacVae."

"Enter!" A woman's voice.

As Danny ushered me in, for a moment I thought I was back home in Edinburgh in somebody's secondhand bookshop again. There were books everywhere, spilling, tumbling, heaped on the windowsills and stacked high against the ceiling. The result was that there wasn't any hope of getting much light into the room.

I suppressed a sigh. My father, so orderly and neat by nature, would have had a fit to see books so ill-used. For him even the most humble and shabby paperbacks were precious.

As for Mrs. MacVae, I didn't expect my presence to be met by open arms, but the woman sitting by the fire put down her book and clapped her hands. "And who is this you've brought us this time, Danny?"

So there were other times. Maybe I wasn't the first to turn down his handsome offer of being with him in the van for the night.

I looked at him quickly but before he could explain, Mrs. MacVae laughed delightedly. "Well, well. Come in, my dear. We've been expecting you. Jetta will be so pleased to know the sea didn't get you after all—Jetta, come and see who we have here."

There was movement in the room on the other side of the fireplace.

"Jetta, come along." The old woman sounded impatient. You could hear the former schoolteacher in her voice as she peered at me as if I might dissolve into thin air before her daughter appeared.

Behind her, Danny made a solemn face, touched his forehead, and mouthed, "She's harmless."

The door from the bedroom opened to admit a younger woman. She walked slowly, using the doorpost and the furniture as support.

She was very pale and if it had been possible to faint clean away, she looked as if she would have done so. As she clutched the back of the nearest chair, her knuckles showed white. Her face couldn't go any whiter. Instead, she went a delicate shade of pale green. At last she got a good look at me.

"See who it is—it's Bridie Ann!" said her mother.

I had gone suddenly cold. As I tried to work it out, I hardly listened to Danny's introductions, to his explanation for my presence and that I needed a room.

I was still shaken but perhaps a little less than Jetta. Whatever had scared the wits out of her when we met, she now had the situation in hand. In a voice quite normal she said, "Of course, you can have a room."

As Danny chatted to Mrs. MacVae, she made an attempt at a smile and whispered, "Take no notice of Mother, she's a bit wandered these days. She lives for her books—not quite in the real world, if you know what I mean."

She sighed and shook her head sadly, then turned quickly to Danny. "What was that you were asking?"

"Just if it's all right—for Annie to stay."

"Of course. And we'll take good care of your friend, won't we, Mother?" And to me she said, "If you'll just give us a little time to prepare a room. Come back later, perhaps." Then as Danny led the way to the door, she said, "We only do bed and breakfast; we don't do an evening meal."

That smile again that never once touched her eyes, scared and watchful. "I suppose Danny has told you, we don't usually hire out rooms except—for friends of friends, you know—so there will be a very small charge." The amount she was asking was so small that I decided I'd insist they take twice as much, if only for the breakfasts involved.

Walking down the path, Danny laughed. Seeing my expression, he said anxiously. "I hope I did right."

"What do you mean?"

"I hope I haven't let you in for something."

I frowned. "I don't understand."

Danny was leading the way toward the path and his van. He turned, smiled at me, and shook a finger. "I think you do, Annie."

"I haven't the slightest idea what you're talking about."

He just smiled and said nothing. There was a fierce wind blowing on the cliff face and we needed all our breath to climb the short distance to the van.

Once inside, I took a seat by the window and watched him brew fresh coffee. The smell was delicious. "I'll take you down to the hotel for supper—I may have to make it myself. Depends on what they have in the freezer. But meanwhile, make yourself at home."

Sitting alongside, he said, "Well, aren't you going to tell me what all this is about?"

I shook my head, grateful for the coffee. I needed it.

Danny grinned, pointed to the mug I was holding between my hands. "Nothing to say, eh?"

I shrugged, took a sip, and tried not to let my hands shake.

Danny was not to be put off. "Come on, Annie Kelty. Your hands are saying it all."

"What do you mean, saying it all?"

"Well, for one thing, you're nursing that mug like someone who has just survived a rail crash or a national disaster. For another, you were terrified out of your wits down there. Quite honestly, I didn't know which one— Jetta or yourself—I was going to have to scrape off the floor first. You both looked ready for the kiss of life!"

He paused, giving me a chance to say something. When I just stared into the depths of the coffee mug, he said gently, "Your name, wasn't it? Them knowing it. Why did that scare you so much? I realize you've never set foot in these parts before." So he had guessed.

And I told him that here was one of my best-kept secrets. "The name on my birth certificate, the name I never ever used because I was mocked at school—a bridie is a pastry from the bakery—" I stopped.

"I know what a bridie is. I'm a chef, for heaven's sake," he added sharply. "Go on!"

"Well, only on the most official of documents am I reminded that I was baptized Brida Ann Kelty."

Danny whistled. "And yet the name she called you was Bridie Ann."

I looked at him. I still didn't know what to say or where to begin. I had an idea that the easy lie wouldn't work with Danny. Somehow, somewhere in his life, he'd been there and done it all.

He stretched out a hand and grasped mine across the table. A warm, strong, comforting hand. "Tell me, Annie. Who knows, perhaps I can help."

I took a deep breath. "Bridie Ann was my mother's name too—"

The next minute I was telling him the whole story—everything, nightmares and all, the terrible fear that she had died because of me. That I might have killed her. Knowingly or by some horrible accident, I was responsible for her death.

And all this dreadful tale of woe, of terror that I had never breathed to a soul before. As I heard myself talking, I couldn't believe it. I couldn't stop either. It was like some wild waterfall of words and fears pouring out of me. I was telling all, baring my innermost feelings, to a stranger.

In a couple of days, we'd go our separate ways. We'd never meet again. Or so I thought.

At the end of my story, he didn't say anything for a while, just giving me enough time to decide: He thinks

I'm crazy. I was wishing I could unsay it all when he smiled. "So what makes you certain your mother had some link with Stormer?"

"Quite by chance I saw a photo of my father in a group of servants who worked at a castle in Loch Roy. I was doing a job for my father," I added hastily, not wanting to bring Dad's activities into this any more than was strictly necessary.

"I was told that he had been courting one of their servants, had married her, and had gone to Stormer. The man who told me didn't know any details except that it had ended in tragedy."

Danny shrugged. "So what? A lot of marriages do."

"Don't you understand? Tragedy suggests death and disaster and is most probably the reason why my father won't discuss her with me."

Danny nodded slowly. "So you've got it into your head that you were to blame."

"That's right."

"Annie, there could be a lot of reasons, not one of them concerning you," he added gently. "And nothing to do with Stormer."

"I don't know about that. But the way those two at the manse reacted makes me certain that they knew her."

He nodded. "You have a point there. Anyway, you'll be sure to get something out of Martha MacVae to make your journey worthwhile." He grinned. "She loves gossip."

Suddenly solemn, he said, "Something, I hope, to end all those bad dreams." He paused and said gently: "Are you hungry?"

I felt washed out, emptied by this tale of old wounds and high emotion. "I don't feel like a big dinner in your hotel."

"Neither do I. I do a neat line in scrambled eggs. How about that?"

I watched him cooking as I set the table. It all seemed familiar as if I'd done it all before, mostly I suppose because everything was near to hand. It wasn't in the least like working in someone else's kitchen.

He must have been a superb chef, I thought. He worked neatly with great speed, completely absorbed by the task in hand. We hardly talked at all. I was glad because I'd talked myself out completely.

"Enjoy!" he said and set the plates in front of us. The eggs were delicious. A simple dish turned into a banquet by a bottle of wine.

We talked of ordinary things, books we had liked, TV soaps, Edinburgh and the Festival. It was as if I had never poured out my soul an hour ago. We had turned back into strangers again—meeting for the first time.

The wine was very good, a chef's choice. Danny wouldn't snatch up any old bottle from the market to keep in his van. He wouldn't insult even the humblest meal with a cheap wine. I knew that much about him at the same time as I saw that the bottle was empty and my face was feeling rather warm.

Danny was smiling at me gently across the table. He took my hand and held it.

I didn't protest. It was growing dark outside. "I'd better go," I said and stood up, releasing his hand, fighting to break out of the spell cast over us by this small and perfect setting for romance. Some casual talk would do—anything—like the dogs I had heard barking outside as we ate.

"Does someone keep hounds around here?"

He shook his head. "Not that I know of. Fancy a little

blood sports, do you? I can lend you a rifle to play with," he added mockingly.

"Of course, I don't want to shoot anything and I'm dead against fox hunting. It's just the dogs barking out there. I suppose someone has kennels nearby."

Danny stared at me. "Kennels? Dogs?" Suddenly he roared with mirth. "Those aren't dogs, Annie. They're seals—down there on the rocks. They start barking at this time every night. Sounds just like dogs, doesn't it?"

He shrugged. "To tell the truth, I never notice them. They're just a part of the scenery, like the seabirds and the rabbits. That's what the rifle's for, by the way. The hotel thought rabbit pie might go down well on the menu—cheap too. But I never had the heart to kill them or the stomach to skin them either."

We were at the door and he helped me into my jacket. Suddenly his arms were around me, touching my breasts.

I shrugged myself away from him. "No, Danny," I said firmly.

"You wouldn't like to change your mind and stay here?"

"No, Danny."

He smiled. "Pity." He looked at me. "You love this guy you've left back at Airdbenn, best man at the wedding? No chance of him being second-best—just for a little while?" he whispered.

"No chance at all. I'm going to marry him, Danny. I don't play around and he's not going to play second fiddle in this scenario."

He laughed and staggered back, a hand to his heart. "You got me there!"

I wasn't smiling so he shook his head sadly. "A pity, Annie. What a waste of what might have been."

We walked down toward the village where the noise of the seals covered the silence between us. "Are they always like this?" I asked, thinking I wasn't in for much sleep at this rate.

"This is Lammastide. It's the annual seal gathering. Martha MacVae will tell you all about it. She's great on folklore."

At the gate of the manse, he turned to me. "Any plans for tomorrow?"

When I said I hadn't thought that far ahead, he nodded. "I'll come for you at ten. Help with your research—unless you want to be alone."

I couldn't think of a good or even a bad excuse to offer. My attack of virtue was beginning to make me feel foolish. How many other girls would have refused the offer to sleep with Danny, I wondered. I felt like a prim and nervous virgin, which I wasn't and hadn't been for a long time.

But I had a man in my life. I loved him and I was going to marry him.

And I was to repeat those words over and over in the days that followed. They became like some sort of a charm as I tried to resist Danny and stay faithful to Calum.

CHAPTER 5

As I went into the manse, the sitting room looked more than ever like a bookshop that had been swept through by a tornado. Mrs. MacVae was seated in its midst at a round table, a book opened before her under a table lamp. I felt candles would have been more appropriate. The setting didn't even set foot in this century.

Laying aside the book, she offered to show me to my room. I followed her up a once grand oak staircase and felt quite hopeful about my bedroom since the book invasion ended on the landing halfway upstairs.

My hopes were in vain. The bedroom doors in their original wood looked promising, but these rooms were not for me. Martha led the way up another flight of stairs, narrow and steep, added by some later occupant of the manse. These were the attics, by tradition the servants' quarters.

She led the way into a bedroom with a low ceiling, but with a large skylight window staring across the sea toward a silver horizon dotted with the strange hump-backed islands. The old-fashioned bed had snow-white covers, clean and comfortable-looking and at that moment, very inviting.

She pointed to my backpack, which I'd brought up from the hallway. "If you'd like to come downstairs when you're ready, we usually have a cup of hot chocolate at nine."

That seemed like a good idea. I had a feeling I should begin my search by chatting with Martha MacVae. I guessed that we were both curious about one another, dying to find answers to a lot of questions.

When I went downstairs for my nightcap, there was a plate of scones on the table with homemade jam and cream—a nice dessert to my egg dish earlier.

"And how is Danny?" she asked as if she hadn't seen him for some time.

"Oh, just fine," I said as if he were a mutual buddy with whom we shared many happy memories.

She buttered a scone thoughtfully. "An old friend, is he?"

"No, I haven't know him very long," I said cautiously. "We met at a friend's wedding."

She raised her eyes heavenward. "Oh, so romantic."

I wondered if I should at this stage introduce Calum into the conversation, but she went on. "I'm so glad he brought you to visit us." And hesitantly, "There isn't a lot of room in that caravan of his. Not that I've been inside myself, but I do know that there can't be much room for lady guests."

She paused and gave me a severe schoolteacher-like glance. "We do not approve of the goings-on of young

people these days. Even engaged couples. We feel that it is
only right and proper that they wait until they are married."

I said nothing. Proper for some, maybe, but I wasn't
prepared to make any snap judgments on moral themes.

"We are very very fond of Danny," she added severely
as if I might be toying with the idea of leading him
astray. "Such a fine young man."

I felt the time had come to change the subject so I
smiled and said, "The seals are very noisy, aren't they?"

"They are indeed. I hope they don't keep you awake.
We get so used to it, we never notice. But strangers find
it a little disturbing. They are very busy at Lammastime.
They all gather from the ocean for miles and miles
around, like some sort of annual convention. Are you
interested in seals? Do you care for animals? Does their
future worry you?" she added anxiously.

I said yes, and that was true. I cared deeply about the
future of all living creatures as well as the earth we are
privileged to live on.

She liked that. After a moment's pause to let me have
a couple of bites of scone, she said, "What brought you to
Stormer—apart from seeing Danny, that is?" She smiled.
"He doesn't usually bring any of his friends. In fact, you
must be the very first he has brought since he rented the
caravan earlier this year."

Danny's activities didn't seem any reason for surprise,
but she went on. "It did seem strange to us that such an
attractive, lively young man should wish to spend so
much time in this quiet place. We don't have anything to
interest him, not even a library. We have to go to the
other village halls for concerts and plays.

She gave a sad shake of the head. "Stormer wasn't
always like this. The old people of my parents'
generation say there is a curse on it. The seal folk, you

know. They always bring ruin to humans who invade what has been their territory since the beginning of time. They pay homage to the sea gods. Christianity means little to them."

"Is that why the church is a ruin?" I didn't believe a word of it, but she took me seriously.

She gave me an admiring glance. "Of course. You just have to look around you at all the ruined crofts, and you'll know that the kingdom of the sea is what we frail mortals have to contend with. Humans have been given grave warning long ago and man would have disappeared if we hadn't been determined to hang on and respect the sea gods. And of course, we chose ministers who understood and were kind to the seals."

I was amused at a woman of her intelligence, a former schoolteacher, believing in such nonsense. "What about Stormer Hall? Was the owner not kind to seals either?" I asked.

She shook her head solemnly. "There was a curse on him and all his kind. He didn't belong to Stormer or understand the rules."

I wanted to know more about that lost and lonely mansion and its owners, but at that moment, the door opened and Jetta came in. I was glad she smiled calmly at me and I no longer terrified her.

Even close at hand, her face turned neither white nor pale green this time but stayed a perfectly normal color. In fact, she looked as if she hadn't a care in the world as we talked about Edinburgh and the weather. Her mother cut short this rather dull topic.

"Jetta, I've just been telling Miss Kelty that she is very like someone we used to know. A pupil of mine—"

This was news to me. Had I been asleep and missed that bit? I smiled politely, waiting for some explanation.

Jetta's composure was gone. She looked very scared. Her knuckles went white and for a moment I thought I was in for a dramatic color change again. Matters weren't helped by her mother nodding across at me and saying loudly, as if her daughter weren't present, "She went off with Jetta's man, you know." It was said with such malicious glee that I felt sorry for Jetta.

For a moment I had a glimpse of the rather unpleasant home life that existed between Martha MacVae and her daughter.

Jetta recovered and whispered, "That was a very long time ago, Mother."

Mrs. MacVae shook her head. "But you have a very long memory, Jetta dear, don't you?" She sighed. "Oh well, haven't we all. And poor Bridie paid for her sins, that's for sure. The sea washed her clean—"

"Mother!" said Jetta sharply. "Please. I'm sure Miss Kelty doesn't want to hear all about past history," and turning to me, she asked, "How's Danny?"

I didn't want to go through all that again, so I said, "He's fine, but I'm not here to see Danny. I came because I'm interested in the local weaving community. We get a lot of their knitwear in our Edinburgh shops."

"Well, well," Martha seemed surprised to hear that.

"I'd like to visit the factory if I can."

"You can see it from your bedroom window. It's that great barnlike place at the end of the village."

"The one with the high fence around it?"

"That's it."

I was disappointed. I didn't want to say its outside didn't suggest a place that created beautiful wools and lovely sweaters.

Martha saw my expression and said, "They weren't

always prosperous. The barn was an army barracks once, built during the Second World War—a jail for prisoners of war and enemy aliens."

"They should have been safe enough here," I said, "Hardly an easy escape to anywhere."

"Only the sea. And for that you need ships." Martha sighed. "The English were always good at finding places to dump things they didn't want. They decided to dump their enemies on us; now they dump their nuclear waste instead."

"The Italian prisoners of war weren't all that bad, Mother," said Jetta. "They were very kind to the children. And the crofters were glad of their help on the farms. The fishermen too. A lot of the lads were simple folk from coastal villages in southern Italy. They were pretty harmless."

I looked at Jetta. That was quite a speech in their defense.

"Harmless!" repeated her mother harshly. "A bunch of robbers, the lot of them!"

"Only three as I remember."

"You remember! How would you know what went on? You were just a wee baby then, forty years ago," was the scornful reply.

I looked from one to the other. One thing was becoming clear in my short stay in this house. There wasn't much love lost between these two women.

"Don't listen to Jetta. There was a gang of them, a sort of Mafia, you'd call it today. There were big houses in the neighboring areas in those days. Quite wealthy people lived in them but when their menfolk were called up, the servants went too. Take Stormer Hall—all they had left was just one daft old caretaker to run the place.

"The Italian prisoners were sent to keep the grounds and the greenhouses in order—work the vegetable gardens and so forth. They worked more than that. In no time at all, they broke into the house and stripped it bare. A great hoard of silver and valuable antiques."

She paused for breath and I asked. "What happened to the valuables?"

Martha shrugged. "Who knows? That's the mystery to this day. They could hardly hide it in the jail while they were waiting for the ringleaders to plan a breakout. They intended taking it with them, escaping back to Italy by enemy submarine, and starting a new life on the proceeds. But one of their gang who'd helped and lost his nerve—maybe he thought he was getting a raw deal or something, so he told the prison guards. It was in all the papers and it didn't do him much good. His mates were shot on the beach while trying to escape. They didn't have the hoard with them. It was never found. It just disappeared completely."

"It would be worth a king's ransom at today's prices," said Jetta, animated for the first time. "I wish we knew where to lay hands on it. A treasure trove!"

"I daresay. The Stormer Hall folk didn't survive the war. The son who had inherited was a widower, lived in London, and was killed in a German air raid. His two sons died in active service."

"That means it would be finders keepers," said Jetta eagerly. "It's probably still buried somewhere in the village just waiting to be found. Just think, we'd all be rich," she added with a giggle.

"I wouldn't bank on it," said her mother acidly.

Pretending not to notice Martha's scornful look, Jetta piled the supper mugs onto a tray and was heading toward the kitchen.

"Let me do that," I said.

She stood by as I rinsed the dishes, as if there were something she would like to say. Then with a shrug she turned away and said, "Well, I'm off to bed. Careful on those stairs," she added, watching me.

It was too dark to read her expression, but I couldn't shake off the feeling of menace. Or was I being too sensitive? Was Jetta's attitude merely envy for anyone who was still young and fit?

From the window I had a better view of the barnlike structure that housed Laverock Knitwear. It did indeed look like a prison camp. I wondered why they hadn't bought Stormer Hall. If they were as prosperous as they seemed to be, it should have been a simple matter to make it livable again. Wealthy people buy ruined castles every day in Scotland and turn them into agreeable homes, helped by grants from local councils and societies who want to preserve historic buildings.

Were the Laverock Knitwear people superstitious? It seemed unlikely that hardheaded businessmen or women would be put off by some ancient legends about selkies— even if all those seals basking on the rocks and barking like dogs did strike a chill into them on cold misty nights.

How did Laverock Knitwear transport their products? Certainly not through the village's one winding street and up that tortuous hill I had traveled on Danny's motorcycle. And Stormer Hall had a private access road, so he told me, to the main Oban route.

Presumably they used a sea route by ferry to the mainland to transport their wool. Tomorrow, all would be revealed and I guessed that there was a very simple solution to that particular problem.

Tomorrow. I was looking forward to a visit to the factory and having all or some of my questions answered.

I yawned. Suddenly weary, the prospect of a good night's rest in that little bed under the eaves was very desirable. And of course, there was an interesting-looking bookshelf, without which no room in this house would ever be complete.

I yawned. Tonight I was too tired to read. To tell the truth, I was almost too tired to wash my face and clean my teeth. The shower cabinet in the tiny bathroom next door to my bedroom gave only a thin stream of ice-cold water.

As I climbed into bed and swung over the sheets, I collided with the shelf above my head. A book flopped down onto the pillow.

I picked it up and was about to replace it when I noticed the rather quaint, faded blue binding. For no reason I could think of, holding it brought a feeling that I had seen it somewhere before, a twitch of memory—

"The Legend of the Seal Woman." The light was poor and there was no bedside reading lamp. I'd ask Martha if I might borrow it to read tomorrow.

The book fell open at the flyleaf and written in a childish hand: "Bridie Ann. Her secret book." What had I stumbled onto? My heart raced—here were secrets indeed!

CHAPTER 6

I felt a wave of excitement. Had I at last stumbled on some clue to Brida Ann, who I was certain was my missing mother?

Martha had said of her onetime pupil, "The sea washed her clean."

So she had drowned? Would the book I held in my hand, written in a childish hand, give me the answer? It fell open at "The Lammas Seal-Man."

"The king of the seals left his kingdom of coral and pearl beneath the waves and at Lammastide, shed his skin and took on the form of a handsome young man. The first woman who sets eyes on him as he rises from the waves falls in love with him and is his slave forever. Although she is ready to follow him to the world's end, he takes her as his wife for only one year and a day. Then when the Seal People call him, he must return to his own again. Endowed with magic, he is irresistible to women.

"This is the true story of Tom Selks."

And there the story ended, to my disappointment. Who was Tom Selks and what part had he played in the life of Brida Ann?

I laid the book to my cheek and sniffed the faded page, as if it might still contain some magic of the girl who had written it. It must be wonderful, I thought, to throw away the world for one man's love, even for a year and a day.

Would I do it for Calum Crail? More sensible—would I do it for any man?

Of course, such madness belonged to a world of fantasy. It was very old-fashioned to belong only to one man for one's whole life. Our Edinburgh friends mostly had many short-term affairs, set up house for a couple of years or less, then drifted off to another love. Their excuse was boredom; their views on sex and on one love for life were very cynical.

I have to confess that I hadn't had any serious lover until I met Calum, although I always pretended to my girlfriends that I had! Living with my father was the main reason, since he had always kept a strict and sharp eye on boyfriends.

Dreams were different. They were beyond his control or mine either. They were strange and wild. Like my dreams that night when I laid aside Brida Ann's book, certain that I'd never sleep a wink.

But sleep I did and the man who walked in my dreams, alas, bore no likeness to Calum Crail! He had black hair and eyes, he was lean and tall, a seal-man with the face of Danny Lucas!

*   *   *

It was eight o'clock when I opened my eyes next morning to the welcome smell of bacon frying downstairs. I leaped out of bed, realizing I was hungry. I tend to forget to eat at regular hours when more exciting things beckon.

As I went downstairs, I saw that the islands had vanished. In fact, everything beyond the garden hedge was hidden behind a thick gray veil of mist. Far away I heard the echo of the seals barking. Instead of dogs they sounded like the cries of humans in distress.

Martha MacVae was in the kitchen, the table set for breakfast.

"Sit ye down, lass. Sorry the weather's not kind to you. We get days like this at Lammastide. Something to do with the heat rising from the land and meeting the cold air offshore. I don't pretend to understand it personally. Teaching science wasn't my subject and no one was fussy about wanting to know how everything worked in my village school. Now the television has all nature's secrets ready to open for everyone who cares to watch them."

And she watched me as I ate, encouraging me to more toast, more coffee, more homemade jam. It was quite a feast!

"What are you going to do today?" she said, looking out of the window. "You won't be able to travel far in this, I'm afraid."

As she stood up to move the plates, she swayed slightly and took hold of the chair for support.

"What's wrong?" I asked in alarm.

She shook her head, tried to straighten up, and groaned. "My angina. Pills are over there on the dresser."

"I'll get them." I took the bottle over to here. There was only one pill left and she put it under her tongue. A moment later she looked better.

She took up the empty bottle and shook it. "I didn't

realize I was almost out of pills. I haven't had an attack
for weeks now." She looked worried.

"Will you be all right?"

"That I don't know, lass. Sometimes I get two or three
attacks with just hours between them and then nothing
for weeks or months." She shook the empty bottle.
"Jetta's away for the day. She'd never think of checking
whether I had my pills. When I don't have an attack for a
while, we always hope that maybe there won't be
another one."

"Look, I can get pills for you down at the village and
bring them back."

She began to protest about being a nuisance and I said,
"It's no trouble. I'm not doing anything else. It's hardly
the day for sight-seeing. I only want to go as far as the
knitting place and buy some yarn."

Martha looked relieved. "If you're sure, I'd be grateful.
It's the doctor you have to get them from; we don't have
a chemist in the village. Too small."

"Right. Where is he?"

I followed her to the window. "Over there." She
pointed in the direction of Danny's van. "Dr. Brackley's
retired now. He lives in the factor's cottage that once
belonged to Stormer Hall. You take the cliff path for
about half a mile and then you come to a gate. You can't
miss it. Tell him I sent you—"

"I don't need a note—a prescription or something like
that?"

Martha laughed. "Dr. Brackley never bothers with such
things. He knows us all well. We've all been his patients
for years and years, since he was a young man, brought
some of us into the world. We're all the family he ever
had. Been a widower for years."

I followed her to the door. The heavy mist had turned into rain.

She looked at my jacket. "Is that all you have with you?"

I said it was. "Best take Jetta's golf umbrella then. Here you are." And from behind the door, she took and unfurled an umbrella striped in red, white, and blue.

At my expression, she laughed. "Take care of it. It's a well-known landmark in Stormer. Everyone knows it!"

Quickly I checked the directions with her. As she pointed out the way once more, I noticed there was no telephone in the hall. "Tell me, what happens if anyone needs a doctor urgently?"

"There's a telephone booth beside the general store."

Not much use if you had a heart attack, I thought, as she went on, "Dr. Brackley has a telephone, of course. And he's very fit. Walking half a mile is nothing to him." She opened the umbrella for me. "I've just thought of something else. When you're out, would you bring some extra milk from the village? Jetta and I don't use much but we're not used to having an extra mouth to feed. You'll need it for your porridge in the morning and your coffee. You can't miss the shop—there's only the general store." And as an afterthought, she said, "Perhaps you wouldn't mind handing it in as you come past on your way to the doctor's. Save carrying it up the hill and back."

I held out my hand. The rain had stopped. "I won't need this now," I said and handed back the umbrella.

"As you wish, but don't rely on it staying dry," she warned.

The walk down to the village shop was chilly and unpleasant. There wasn't much romance about Stormer on a day like this. I was keeping a lookout for the shop and the street was almost deserted except for a woman talking to a young man, the only residents in view. Perhaps the others wisely stayed indoors on such mornings.

The woman wasn't suitably clad for the weather at all. She was wearing a wide-brimmed straw hat as if she were in danger of being sunburnt with her hair tied up in a scarf underneath it. When she turned around, I saw the dark sunglasses almost hiding her face.

But it was her companion who caught my attention. They were about twelve feet away from me and I realized it was Danny she was talking to—

No! A moment later, I realized it wasn't him. Just a young man who looked so much like him at that distance he could have been mistaken for his brother. I nodded politely and said good-day, although it wasn't.

And as I walked past, they glanced in my direction without returning my greeting. Then, intent on their own talk, as if startled by my sudden appearance, they turned away. But when I looked back, I saw that they seemed to be still watching me, their heads together, whispering.

I didn't like it. My first encounter with Stormer's inhabitants and they're hostile.

I fared better in the general store. There were two young women with babies in buggies and they greeted me kindly, saying how awful the weather was. And was I staying long? One of them assured me that this wasn't the kind of weather they usually had here in August.

"Oh, yes, usually we're having lovely, long sunny days by now," echoed her companion.

The woman behind the counter as I paid for the milk also asked if I was staying long. Obviously strangers were something of a novelty.

"Just passing through," I said and she smiled and wished me a pleasant stay.

But I left the store feeling cold and depressed as I made

my way back to Martha MacVae's. The only thing to do on a day like this was to take up a good book or switch on the television, keep warm, have lots to eat, and forget the weather. And at all costs avoid looking out at the swirling mist, which had now changed into more heavy rain.

But easy escape was not for me. I remembered the purpose of my visit to Stormer. Rain or shine, I had little time and I must continue my quest.

Martha met me at the front door. Taking the milk from me, she thrust the umbrella into my hand. "You'll need this now." Her smile said clearer than any words, "I told you so."

As I walked down the path again, she shouted, "Take care now, won't you? That cliff path can be a bit dangerous. Don't go too near the edge or you'll land down in the sea with all the seals."

She found that very amusing. She was still laughing as she closed the door. As I stumbled across the dripping grass toward the cliff, I didn't find it all that funny.

My thoughts kept returning to the woman in the ridiculous, all-concealing sun hat and the young man who looked like Danny. I wondered who he was and why I felt there was something rather sinister about that first encounter in the village. Come to think of it, Martha MacVae was a bit sinister herself, to say nothing of her daughter Jetta.

And as for those seals, barking through the rain, they sounded like tormented souls. I sighed—there weren't going to be many laughs in Stormer!

"It's telling you something, Annie. Rely on your instinct and get away while the going's good. While you still have time. Escape," whispered the still, small voice of reason.

But of course, I didn't. As I was to learn to my peril, I never listened. I never do.

CHAPTER 7

It never occurred to me that the cliff path would actually be dangerous, or that I should heed Martha's warning to take care.

The sea might not have existed at all beyond twenty yards where the mist took over. Even its roar was hushed a little today as if it were subdued by the heavy weight of moisture above it. The rocks gleamed like patent leather and I realized that this must be ebb tide.

Suddenly there was movement—round black heads bobbing about in the sea, as if at some given signal the seals had appeared. They seemed to be staring up at me and it was all rather scary for even at that distance, their heads were like those of human swimmers. They looked like wrinkled old men, which explained why men were so ready to believe in mermaids and seal people.

The strange thing was that they watched me so intently. Their doglike barking was stilled as if—stupid as it sounds—they were brooding over something important, considering their next move, what action to take.

I waved to them and called "Hello!" I know that does sound a bit crazy, but then I always talk to animals I meet in Edinburgh: dogs, cats, and horses, and I thank birds for singing so sweetly. I feel that the pleasure they give shouldn't be taken for granted.

But as I walked along the cliff path, I was curious about those seals and just a little scared, as they took to the water, keeping pace with me as I walked.

Sometimes they paused, like well-trained dogs staring in my direction, waiting politely, as Calum's dog Nero did, for me to catch up with them!

I could almost hear Calum's words. He would shake his head and say, "It was all that empty landscape getting on your nerves. The seals weren't following you—just obeying some natural law of ebb and flood tide."

Calum is clever about such things. He is very good at logic, which is quite beyond me. I listen with a polite smile, pretend to take it all in, even throw in some interested remarks, but I don't understand any of it really.

The silence that wrapped itself around me as I walked was like a shroud, cold and clammy. I wasn't used to this absence of people, this sudden isolation.

Then I saw that I was mistaken. There on the shore was a figure bending over one of the rock pools. It was the strange lady with the sun hat. I wondered what she was searching for and how she could see anything through dark glasses on a day like this.

She must have sensed that she was being watched. She straightened up and looked across at the cliff path, obviously wondering who was under the big umbrella and finding her movements so interesting.

I waved and shouted, "Hi!" Either she didn't hear or didn't want to. She turned back to her task of searching the rock pool.

Weird, I thought. This is hardly the day I would have chosen to gather seaweed or shells. The rain had stopped but the cliff path was steeper now with plenty of small rocks, nicely placed to turn the ankle of an unwary traveler. I doubted if anyone would be eager to take this path in darkness or bad weather.

As I turned a corner away from the sea, the wind was suddenly fierce. I stopped, looking for the gate to the doctor's house. Could I have missed it in the fog?

But suddenly, there it was. Getting it open was another matter. I pushed and shoved to no avail. Obviously visitors or patients used the wobbly stile in the stone wall, which also showed signs of neglect.

I clambered over, followed a graveled path, and twenty yards farther along I saw the tiny croft, the retirement home of the village doctor.

Ringing the bell brought no immediate response, so I tried again and kept my finger on it this time. As I waited I hoped again that no one ever wanted a doctor in a hurry and had to tackle that cliff path to seek his help.

At last the door opened and a very old man leaning on a cane peered out at me. "Didn't you hear?" he said, sounding rather put out. "I shouted to you to come in. The door's always open," he added severely.

Meeting him face to face was my second reason for hoping the inhabitants were all healthy and not subject to violent accidents. Following him indoors as he limped ahead of me, I saw that he was not only old but infirm, relying on the cane to get around.

"Take a seat," he said without asking me what I'd come for.

"Mrs. MacVae needs some pills for her angina."

"More pills? I gave her daughter some the other week," he said. He looked puzzled and then he shrugged. "Ah, well, I suppose she's just mislaid them. She often does that. Come with me and I'll get you some from the surgery."

The surgery was a room packed with cardboard boxes. The Ministry of Health would have locked it up and stuck a condemned notice on the door.

He must have noticed my expression of dismay as he said apologetically, "They're all my books mostly and some other things I brought with me." He scratched his head and peered at some labels. "Ornaments, china, and crystal in that one. Well, well."

He seemed to have forgotten the object of my visit. "What was it ails you, lass?" he said, looking at me critically over the top of his spectacles. "You're not one of my patients, are you?"

"It's not for me, Doctor. I've come for Martha MacVae's pills."

"Well, well. And what's your name?"

I told him and he nodded. "Keeping in fine shape yourself, are you?"

I wondered if I looked ill. "Fine," I said.

"That's great. Great. Now." He paused and looked at a cupboard with glass door and shelves packed with old-fashioned bottles, all labeled. It was like a scene from a Victorian movie.

What happened to modern medicine, to penicillin and antibiotics, I wondered. Had he ever heard of them? With a cry of triumph, he seized a labeled bottle. Opening it, he took an envelope out of the drawer and counted out some pills.

His hand shook so much that quite a few of them

escaped and fell on the floor unnoticed. From the powdery evidence it looked as if that happened quite often, and they were trampled underfoot.

"Tell her not to lose these ones," he said and added proudly, "What do you think of my little surgery?"

I couldn't readily come up with an answer to that one. I was still in a state of shock. The laboratory in R. L. Stevenson's horror story *Dr. Jekyll and Mr. Hyde* was the first thing that sprang to mind.

"You'll notice that I don't hold with all these modern instant cures," he said sternly.

I looked at him. Perhaps he was a better doctor than I gave him credit for. He seemed to have read my thoughts!

"Nature is still the best cure for all that ails us. That's what God intended. This modern stuff is man being too clever for his own good, paving the way to his own destruction. Out there—"

He stopped and gestured to what remained of a garden seriously in need of weeding. "Out there, you could find the cure for everything."

He waited and I nodded politely, thinking I'd need to do a fair amount of spade work to uncover any medicinal herbs in that particular tanglewood.

"Nearly sixty years I've been in Stormer and I know every blessed plant that grows."

I was suddenly interested but not in his plants. If my mother had once lived here, then he might know something about her. I was wondering how to broach the subject when he asked, "Visiting Martha, are you? A relative, is she?"

I explained that I had been at a friend's wedding and while I was in the area, I decided to have a look at Stormer.

He looked surprised. "What made you choose Stormer?"

"Someone in Edinburgh mentioned it, said it was worth visiting."

He frowned. "I didn't catch your name, miss."

"Annie." On a sudden impulse I added, "Bridie Ann."

Dr. Brackley paused and looked hard at me, rubbing a chin with a sandpaper sound that indicated he was badly in need of a shave. "Is that so, miss? Very unusual name. I saved a child out of the sea with that name long ago."

"You did? How strange!"

"Maybe you'd like to hear about it. Did Martha tell you what happened to Jetta? No. Oh, that's a very interesting story!"

I felt I was getting onto the right track when he said, "Let's sit down, shall we? The leg's not very good today. Perhaps you'd like to hear our bit of folklore. That is, if you aren't in a great hurry."

I wasn't and I knew he was dying to tell me. So I followed him into the kitchen and while he boiled the kettle for coffee, he told me the story of Tom Selks and Jetta. How the Selks family—or those connected with them—seemed doomed to tragedy.

And one name stood out of this story. That of Bridie Ann, who I had every reason to believe was my own mother.

CHAPTER 8

Dr. Brackley settled back comfortably in his chair. "The Selks were the first human settlers in Stormer, seal people with magical powers which they don't always use for good. Poor wee Bridie Ann was doomed from the beginning. No one knew where she came from. Old Tam, Tom's father, was out fishing—or so he said—when he found her in an abandoned boat floating out to sea."

He shook his head, remembering. "A tiny baby—not a stitch on her when they brought her to me. More dead than alive she was. It was touch and go for a while, but I managed to save her life. Afterwards—after what happened, I thought maybe I had been wrong and that I should have let her go back to her own people."

I realized he was talking about the seal people when he went on, "There was no means of knowing who she was, so that she could be returned to her human kin—if they existed, that is. Tam's story accounted for their having a newborn baby in the house. Village gossip hinted that she was old Tam's baby. He was a bad lot where young lasses were concerned. The Selks were a fine-looking lot of men, right enough, so maybe the lasses weren't to be blamed either. It takes two to make a baby.

"Anyway, folks said she was either old Tam's or else she belonged to the seal people, and sensible folk would have packed her off to an orphanage. But I knew things about Tam and Bella. Bella had a bad time bringing their son Tom into the world. I knew he would be her first and last. She was so damaged by the birth I doubted whether she'd carry another. So it was a good thing they had Bridie Ann.

"Tom grew up real handsome, and seal man or not, the lasses all loved him too. Especially clever Jetta MacVae, who went away to college at Glasgow. When she came home that summer, she meant to have Tom, but she was too late and Tom was all set to marry his foster-sister.

"Jetta couldn't let it go. She told Bridie Ann that Tom had been drunk one night when she was last home. That he had had his way with her and when he knew she was having his baby, he would marry her. It was all a lie, of course; there wasn't a baby but she had trapped him with the oldest trick in the world."

The doctor paused. "It was very different about such matters then—not what they show us on the television and in the films these days. But thirty years ago, it was still a sin for a lass to give herself to a lad and for him not to honor her by marriage.

"Bridie Ann was heartbroken and she disappeared from Stormer before the wedding. She wrote to me saying she was happy, working as a servant in some big house in the Highlands. Several years passed until one sad day she was back in Stormer with a husband and a wee lass, come to visit old Tam, who was dying.

"Death was in the air. It was Lammastide, a time feared by the Selks when other mortals feared them too. At old Tam's funeral, young Tom clapped eyes on Bridie Ann and she on him. And it was as if they had never been separated, as if neither of them had ever belonged to anyone else.

"Mad for each other, nothing else—nobody else mattered. It was as if the whole world outside had ceased to exist, and they decided just to vanish.

"Tom had grown up with the seal king legend so he and Bridie Ann planned to take a boat and sail away to one of those islands on the horizon that only the birds and the seals claimed as home.

"It was a bleak prospect that sane folk wouldn't have given a second thought to, but these two were mad, hell-bent on finding some place where they could live together. They thought their secret plans were safe, but someone who followed them everywhere heard it all. Bridie's little lass was always trailing behind them. She adored her mother and would hardly let her out of her sight. Her father, it seemed, had little to do with her. He went fishing most days and didn't seem to understand a child's needs. Tom and Bridie Ann, wrapped up in each other like most adults, weren't aware that children listen and take notice of what is being said. So the girl watched them secretly, and God knows what she saw.

"If she'd been older, she would have kept it to herself, but she ran back and told it all to Jetta. Jetta refused to believe her, gave her a good hiding for telling lies. The child ran off and Jetta followed her. She took her father's rifle that hadn't been used for donkey's years."

He stopped and sighed. "No one is very clear what happened after that. It is believed that she tried to shoot the eloping pair but hit the boat instead, and it sank to the bottom of the sea, taking them both with it. Jetta was found late that night, lying on the beach, senseless, with a bullet wound in her leg."

"What happened to—to the little girl?" I asked.

"She disappeared. There was a search party sent out for her, and she was found wandering, suffering from shock and exposure. Her poor father was horrified and took her away. We never heard from either of them. We never wanted to. It was a chapter that we wished to see closed forever. Jetta still carries the scars and the memory. She was lamed for life."

"Didn't the police investigate the suspected drownings?" I asked.

He laughed at that. "Police! There aren't any at Stormer; the nearest are at Oban. And no one called them in. This was a family matter. There was no need for outsiders in this tragedy. That's the way it's always been."

"But what about the pair who disappeared? Didn't you want to know what happened to them?"

"We knew what happened to them," he said grimly.

"Were their bodies washed ashore?"

"No, no. The sea took them. People here would tell you they got their wish—they went to live in the kingdom of the sea."

He stopped and looked at me. "Drink your coffee, lass. It'll be cold."

I felt stricken, shocked. As he told me the story, all I could think of was that not only had I lost a mother, but somewhere along the line I had lost the chance to know a woman who belonged to fantasy. The woman who brought me into the world had a stranger history than any I had ever known.

Had my father been aware of the legends that surrounded her life? The mystery of her being found newly born, abandoned in a boat drifting in the sea?

I knew what Calum would say when I told him. He wouldn't consider it much of a mystery. As far as he was concerned, this had been a matter for the police.

Babies in boats, missing persons, shooting accidents— or intended murder. All should be neatly recorded in the local police files, he would say. As for that baby in the boat, of course! How Calum would laugh at such nonsense. Like all sensible folk who didn't live in Stormer, he would have not the slightest doubt that Bridie Ann was old Tam's baby and the local legend was a neat way to protect his reputation. Perhaps his wife, desperate for another baby, even suggested it to him.

But as I listened to the doctor's story, I saw it all vividly like a movie that was still happening. For me the years fell away, and I seemed to have drifted back into that other time. I became again the little girl crying, watching my mother and her lover sail away out of my life. And at my side, the demented Jetta, screaming, raising the rifle—

Then turning, with the murder rage in her eyes, to me. Running away, run for dear life! What had really happened in those vital moments missing from the doctor's story? Before the boat sank and Jetta was found bleeding on the beach. And the little girl—me—what dreadful part had I played, so terrible that the nightmare has remained with me for the rest of my life?

The doctor saw me to the door and said how much he had enjoyed my visit. He said if I was to be staying awhile, to be sure to call again. "If you're interested in Stormer's history," he added temptingly.

Thanking him, I started off again down the cliff path,

more confused than ever. An analyst might be the answer when I got back to Edinburgh. They put you under hypnosis and whirl you back to painful times that had been buried below the surface of memory.

I thought back about what memory allowed me to recall. How recently standing on the shore of Loch Roy in the Highlands had brought a dreamlike sense of familiarity. Water, a boat bobbing across the waves to an island. But that was all.

If I was the child who was present on the shore when Jetta MacVae tried to kill my mother and her lover, Jetta was never present in my nightmare. No other person but myself. That dramatic, tragic scene with the rifle was missing.

I was walking carefully now, hugging my umbrella tight against the rain that had begun again. It was going to be even slower going down than it had been coming up.

I'd be glad to see the village street, to set foot on safe ground, for I could not shake off the prickling sense of danger. Once I raised the umbrella to see where I was going, and I caught sight of the sun-hatted woman walking about twenty yards ahead of me.

She turned briefly and saw me. Then the cliff path curved, hiding her from view. But when I reached the corner, she was nowhere to be seen.

I was curious. Had she gone down to the shore again? No, it was empty of all but a few seals who seemed to have lost interest in me. Had she managed to get to the cliff top? Where had she gone?

No matter. My main object was to get off this path as quickly as possible. And I was grateful to be out of the wind where the umbrella and I could walk, or scramble, without being blown out to sea!

I thought of Calum. I must try and call him. He might be in Oban by now. Poor Calum. Too late I was feeling guilty about leaving him with a hangover. I should have stayed.

It had been a fool's errand to follow an impulse to go to Stormer where I had believed, quite wrongly, that the truth about my mother would be ready waiting for me. Instead it was as obscure as ever, like trying to find one pebble in all those rocks down on the shore.

And then for no reason at all, I began to think of Danny. I had a sudden longing to see him again, to laugh and flirt with him. To be lighthearted and escape from the weight of sad, old family feuds and long-lost tragedies. I wanted to enjoy this brief episode and with Danny I would be safe!

Why on earth should I think about safety? The path widened slightly at this point and there was a faint overhang of cliff. On an impulse I decided to take a breather. It was an impulse that saved my life.

As I stepped back, a huge rock hurtled down and bounced off the path where I had been walking a moment ago. I heard it smashing away against the rocks down to the shore. I crouched back against the cliff face, terrified to make a move as I waited for more rocks to fall.

There were none, but suddenly there were stealthy movements above me, soft, scraping sounds. Human sounds of footsteps swishing through wet grass. I was rooted to the spot. This single rock hurtling down was no accident. Someone had tried to kill me!

CHAPTER 9

Someone had tried to kill me! Of that I had not the least doubt as I rushed down the hill, trailing the umbrella behind me as if a pack of demons were at my heels. No longer caring about the stony, uneven ground, I risked turning my ankle or falling, conscious only that I must get to the road into the village. Only then would I be safe.

At last I stumbled breathless into the main street. Everything was so normal: there were two women gossiping, another pushing a baby buggy, a man walking a dog. Two old men were smoking pipes, leaning on a wall, staring out to sea.

The weather had changed and a sudden burst of sunshine made the buildings glisten as if there were diamonds studded into their gray walls. As I ran up the path to the manse, it was no longer gloomy, basking in the cozy warmth of a summer morning with insects buzzing among the garden's wildflowers and seeds.

Martha was sitting by the window knitting. She smiled as I came in. "I see the rain's stopped, Annie. You've brought the sun with you. You must be lucky."

As I handed her the pills, I wondered if she would have thought I was so lucky if I had been carried in dead or found lying on the pebbled beach with my neck broken.

Death by misadventure would have been recorded, I thought. There would have been no inquiry. The doctor had told me that they didn't involve the police if they could help it. Such happenings on the island were regarded as family matters and sudden deaths were quickly smoothed over.

It wasn't very consoling for any stranger who might be passing through and have a nasty accident. I went prickly all over when, in the safety of Martha's book palace, I thought of my narrow escape.

"I hope you didn't get too wet," she said. "It's a grand walk on a nice day. Very good for one. I used to do it myself nearly every day until my legs got too bad. Even Jetta manages quite well with her stick."

As I listened in silence, I began to think perhaps I had dreamed the whole thing. Perhaps in my usual fashion, as Calum would call it, I was imagining things.

"Thank you for the pills. I'm much obliged. I mustn't delay you if you have things to do," she said wistfully, "but I would love a cup of tea, Annie. If you don't mind—before you go. And there are some nice fresh scones Jetta baked. We might have one of those each."

At her direction I found kettle and teabags and was putting the cups on a tray when the door opened and Jetta came in.

"Another cup, dear," called Martha. "Gracious, Jetta, you are out of breath. And where have you been since breakfast?"

"Just walking."

"Just running by the look of you," said her mother. "You left me on my own—without my pills too. If it hadn't been for Annie here, I don't know what I would have done, really I don't."

Her voice took on a whining note and Jetta said, "What do you mean, without your pills?"

"I had to ask this kind girl here to get me some from the doctor—she had to go all that way in the rain too."

"Mother! You have plenty of pills." Jetta went to a drawer, opened it, and took out a small bottle. She shook it. "Look! There are at least ten pills here!"

"Oh, are there?" Martha said sweetly. "Then I must have been looking in the wrong place," she added. Not a word of apology for all the trouble she had put me to, either.

"Indeed you were," said Jetta. And turning to me she said, "Mother sometimes forgets where she puts things these days."

"What do you mean?" Martha cut in angrily. "I have all my faculties, I'll have you know, which is more than I can say of you."

"All right, then tell me where you put your checkbook yesterday. And how many times I have to search for your glasses—"

The two women glared at each other across the room. I could feel a real big domestic brawl brewing up. I didn't want to be involved. I'd been there too many times at home, arguing with Dad.

I decided to make myself scarce. They hardly paused long enough to hear my cheerful, "Well, I must be going." And I went!

The first person I saw walking along the street was Danny—or was it? As I called out to him, I wondered for a moment if he had heard me or if it was his look-alike again.

Then he turned. "Annie! I was coming to look for you. Come on, I'll treat you to a coffee."

He took my arm and I felt comforted and safe again. I thought we'd be going to the hotel, but the general store had a few plastic tables through a screened-off door with a notice: "Teas, coffee, and ices."

We had the place to ourselves. A girl came to attend to us and Danny gave her that bold look handsome men deliver to waitresses along with their order. In anyone else but Danny—or Calum, of course—it said, "I'm doing you a great favor, honey."

This girl wasn't impressed. Listening silently, she avoided eye contact with him, and her manner was sulky. She didn't like him much, but why was none of my business. Besides, I was dying to tell him of my near disaster on the cliff path. I didn't want to start on it until the coffees came, so in reply to his question about whether I had slept well, I said, "Yes, fine. It's very comfortable. Thank you for finding it for me."

"Did Martha find a corner for you among all those books?"

I laughed. "I've never seen so many!"

"Here's your coffee," said the waitress. And as she was turning away, she said to Danny, "There was a guy in asking for you."

Danny looked surprised. "Oh, when was that?"

She shrugged. "Earlier this morning."

"Did you tell him where to find me?" He sounded cautious.

"I didn't know you were back. I told him to ask at the hotel."

"Thanks!" He sounded relieved and as she went back

into the main shop, he said, "I expect it was someone about a gig. I get asked to play the fiddle at lots of dances, parties, and so forth."

"Do you have a twin by any chance?"

He looked startled. "Me? No! I'm all alone in the world." Puzzled, he added, "Why do you ask that?"

"Because I saw a fellow in the village this morning and for a moment I thought it was you." I laughed. "At first glance, anyone could have mistaken him for you—"

At his doubtful look, I added, "Honestly, Danny. He was your image. I wonder if he was the one who was asking the girl where he could find you."

Danny said nothing and didn't even laugh when I said, "A long-lost cousin, perhaps, come to tell you about a rich uncle who has died in Australia."

"I doubt that. He doesn't sound like anyone I know. More coffee?"

I said no and thought I would be much more curious if I had a look-alike in Stormer. Danny changed the subject by asking, "And what have you been doing all morning?"

"I had to go to the doc for some pills for Mrs. MacVae."

"You mean you had to tackle the cliff path—in that downpour?"

"Oh, it was all right. I had an umbrella."

"The good doctor is quite a character, isn't he?"

"Yes, he certainly is. Full of folklore."

I left it at that. I didn't feel I wanted to go through all the story of Bridie Ann yet again. Later perhaps, but at that moment I saw through the screen the woman with the sun hat and dark glasses going around the shelves, carrying a wire basket.

I had to find some excuse to talk to her. After all, she

was the only person I had seen on the cliff path when I was attacked. Perhaps she had seen something.

"What's the problem?" asked Danny as I stood up.

"I'll be back in a moment."

He nodded, guessing wrongly that I was in urgent need of going to the ladies' room.

I seized a pack of chocolate cookies from the nearest shelf and headed over to the counter where the sun-hatted woman was paying for her groceries. I had just reached it when a girl with a baby buggy and a screaming infant, its face bright red with crying, rushed in front of me.

"You don't mind, do you—please? I'm in a terrible hurry."

As the child's screams were deafening and everyone was staring at her, I could hardly refuse. I decided to put back the cookies and head after the woman who had paid her bill and was walking toward the door.

Unfortunately, the shopkeeper saw me and, giving me a stern look, she shouted rather crossly, "I'll attend to you in a moment, miss. Just wait until I finish serving this lady." The delay was only a couple of minutes but by the time I got out of the shop, my quarry had disappeared.

I thought about it. Probably just as well. What was I going to ask her? I could hardly say, "Excuse me. We haven't met before. I saw you on the cliff path ahead of me a short while ago. Would you mind telling me why you were trying to kill me?"

So I went back into the tearoom where Danny was finishing his coffee, sitting very still and frowning, lost in thought. In fact, he seemed startled to see me again. He looked up. "I saw you in the shop. Where have you been? I thought you were going to dash off and leave me without a word."

"I wouldn't do that, Danny. Honest! I had a reason—"

Maybe there's something wrong with my sense of drama, but I felt he was only half-listening and not all that interested in Dr. Brackley's fascinating account of the seal people. Once he yawned as if he were wondering what was the point of all this and why was I taking all day to get there.

"I know the legend about the Selks family and the baby in the boat, Annie. Everyone does and Dr. Brackley treats all visitors to the full version." His tone warned that he was rather bored.

"Danny, when I was coming back along the cliff path, someone tried to kill me."

He stared at me. "You're joking, of course."

"I am not!"

"Annie—"

"Listen—if a great rock hurtled past you just as you'd stepped off the path, and then you heard a sound like footsteps in the long grass above your head, wouldn't you be just a teeny bit suspicious?"

He shook his head. "There are rockfalls quite often. The cliff face is eroding away with all that rain."

"This wasn't a rockfall, Danny. This was one single, mighty boulder. Big enough to send me flying off the path if it had hit me. I heard it bouncing all the way down to the shore and but for my guardian angel, I'd have been with it." Ignoring his cynical expression, I said, "And what about those footsteps I heard?"

"Annie, I know you got a terrible scare—anyone would. But those footsteps were most likely some grazing sheep straying to the edge. In fact, the same sheep might have dislodged a rock."

"Oh, no, Danny. There was someone up there," I said

triumphantly. "There was a woman I'd seen on my way to the doctor's. She was down at the rock pools gathering shells or seaweed. I waved to her politely but she ignored me. And on the way back she was walking a little ahead of me. But when I reached the bit where the path curves around, there was no sight of her. She had disappeared."

"No, she hadn't, Annie. There are lots of small paths, sheep tracks up to the top of the cliff that the locals know—"

"Thank you, sir. That piece of evidence completes my case."

"What do you mean?"

"Isn't it obvious? She climbed the path without my seeing her and then threw a rock down at me."

Danny sighed and drummed his fingers on the table. "Annie, you haven't been in Stormer twenty-four hours yet. No one knows who you are, so why on earth should anyone have reason to want to kill you? It just isn't logical unless you met some local madwoman who hates strangers."

He paused and thought about that.

"Well," I said. "Any ideas?"

He shrugged. "No, of course not," he said hastily.

"This woman I saw looked, well—quite weird. I'd seen her earlier in the village before I went to the doctor's. As a matter of fact, she was talking to your look-alike—"

"What do you mean, my look-alike?"

"The dark-haired fellow that I thought was you from the distance."

Danny shook his head and gave a rather irritated shrug. "Do you think they were there hatching a plot to kill you? How did they know you would be conveniently walking on the cliff path?" he added mockingly.

When I didn't reply, he said, "Oh, come on, Annie. You've seen too many crime movies. This sort of thing doesn't happen in real life, you know."

I was on familiar ground. This was exactly the way I would have expected Calum to respond to my story. I was furious and hurt. I had expected Danny to be different.

"Tell me about this woman," he said.

"She was very odd. For one thing, she was wearing a big straw sun hat and had all her hair tucked up in a scarf. And big dark glasses. Don't you think that's rather strange? There was no sun. It's been raining, Danny. She looked as if she didn't want to be recognized, as if she might have something to hide," I added triumphantly.

Danny roared with laughter. "Annie, Annie. You had me fooled for a moment. Do you know, I was almost beginning to believe you? I thought it might be—" He stopped and shook his head. "So you think the lady in the sun hat might be your attacker?"

"I think there's a strong possibility," I said as I looked at him very sternly.

"And the motive?"

"Oh, I don't know—a mad impulse."

Danny considered this for a moment, trying to keep a straight face. Then leaning over the table, he took my hand. "Dear Annie, the woman you're describing—" he paused, so overcome with mirth he could hardly speak. "The woman in the sun hat is the very rich, very eccentric owner of our local industry—Laverock Knitwear. Now, why on earth should she want to kill you?"

CHAPTER 10

"Come on, Annie," Danny repeated. "Give me one good reason Mrs. Laverock should want to kill you."

I shook my head. I was baffled and Danny raised a mocking eyebrow. "Is there something you haven't told me? Are you an angry customer whose sweaters have shrunk, or did the colors run?"

"I don't even knit," I said indignantly. "One of my reasons for coming here was to get some yarn for my best friend in Edinburgh." I paused. "It doesn't make sense, does it?"

Seen in this tearoom with people buying groceries and going about their business, with the sun shining outside, the events of the morning seemed to belong to a nightmare. That rainy cliff path, the seals, the wind tearing at my umbrella—it was difficult to believe all these things were happening on the same planet!

If I had needed convincing, then Danny's manner told

me how stupid my suspicions were. I could see that he had decided this was a silly hysterical woman he had on his hands—one he had better treat very carefully.

I felt bad about that. I wanted him to like me, but I could feel that the good impression I had made was going down like a lead balloon.

"Mrs. Laverock has very valid reasons for being on shore at low tide," he said. "She collects seaweed for the dyeing process. She's very proud of the fact that she uses pure wool and natural dyes just as folk did before we entered the plastic age."

"It was the weird garb that fooled me."

"I agree. It takes a little getting used to. As a matter of fact, we don't see her all that often in the village. She rather shuns the social scene."

"Surely a sun hat and dark glasses on a rainy day is going a bit far," I said.

"It goes with her conservation image, taking great care not to encounter any damaging rays from the sun."

"Has anyone ever seen what she looks like?"

"I haven't, but then I'm just a passing stranger too. There could be lots of reasons why she adopts that mode of dress and none of them sinister in the least."

"Name one!" I demanded.

"Maybe she has facial scars, or has gone bald, or had a bad facelift. There could be loads of cosmetic reasons and there's three for a start. And here's another one: I seem to remember someone telling me at the hotel that there was a pretty awful fire a few years ago that destroyed part of the factory."

He shrugged. "Who knows—maybe she tried to rescue some of their precious equipment. Anyway, I've given you four reasons, and I dare say the good doctor could produce another four. There's nothing much happens in Stormer that he doesn't know about or can't ferret out if he puts his mind to it. People confide in doctors."

He looked at his watch. "I have to go now. Someone to see at the hotel about a gig. Can you make your own way back without any rocks falling on you?"

"Oh, that was nasty!"

His smile melted my heart. "Wasn't meant to be, darling, just a piece of concern for a maid in distress, although I'm hardly a knight in shining armor." To me, just then, that was exactly what he was.

As we went outside, the sun was still shining, warm with not a cloud in the sky.

"What are you doing for the rest of the day?" he asked.

"Exploring—my favorite hobby in strange places. I want to look at the old ruined church."

"Nothing much to see there."

"All right, then I'll head to the Laverock place and see if they have Susie's yarn in stock."

He grinned. "Sounds like one exciting day," he said mockingly and then added, "See you around then." He began to walk away without even a handshake. There was something final in the way he moved and I panicked.

What had I done? I would never see him again. And I was filled with regret for opportunity lost. Maybe if I hadn't had any scruples about being engaged to Calum and accepted his offer of staying in the van, he wouldn't just turn his back and walk away from me like that.

Again it was as if he read my thoughts. I was still watching him when he turned and walked back. "Sorry, I forgot. I've got other things on my mind just now, but don't we have a date this evening?"

We didn't but he was smiling deep into my eyes. "Is that still on, Annie?"

I laughed. "I thought you'd never ask!"

He saluted me gravely. "I'll be back at the van at six. Take care and be good now. Don't talk to any strangers."

I left Danny feeling pretty good. He certainly made my heart beat a little faster. I knew I shouldn't, but I set aside my feelings of guilt. I told myself I still loved Calum and wanted to spend the rest of my life with him and I'd be faithful until death do us part. From the day I married him. But at that moment the rest of my life seemed like a long time ahead, and I guessed I might never have the chance to meet anyone as exciting as Danny Lucas again once the wedding vows were said.

Something told me to be cautious, that Danny wasn't husband material. I decided that was why I fancied him so much, because he wasn't in the marriage stakes. There's always a challenge about something you know you want and can never have.

And that summed up Danny nicely. It was obviously that he had no shortage of girls in his life but he had it all under control, walking carefully without getting too involved with any of them. An observer always looking in on himself, like an actor in a stage role.

I guessed that Danny would remain free as air unless his luck ran out and he met the love he was ready to die for. Although I told myself to be sensible about this, a tiny voice inside said, "It could be you, Annie Kelty."

Such were my thoughts as I made my way to the other end of the town and the huge building that housed Laverock Knitwear. As I walked up the path, it was still obvious that this had once been an army barracks or a prison camp. Not even a few shrubs and a few modern additions could conceal the grimness of its original purpose.

I went through the glass doors into a large, richly carpeted reception area with more trees in pots. It looked like the entrance to a smart hotel until you noticed all the photographs on the walls of models showing off the latest designs.

No expense had been spared on building a luxury atmosphere. The room smelt of some perfume that managed to conjure up the wild sea, the pure air. And it added up to a warning about how expensive these garments were going to be.

Gazing in awe through the non-reflective glass at the exquisite show, I did give some thought to the average size of customers like myself. I wondered why they used sticklike models to display their enormous sweaters. The sweaters certainly looked great on the models, but they would make any normal-sized woman look like a barrel on tiny legs.

There were further examples of sweaters Susie would have died for. The patterns were alongside, but I realized however cleverly they were knitted, the result would never be the same and the finished garment would never match up to the one on the model.

"Can I help you?" asked the girl at the desk.

"Please." I produced the swatches of color Susie had given me. "I need to match these."

"Can't you order these through the usual supplier to your shop?"

"I don't have a wool shop. I'm a customer."

She frowned. "This is most unusual for us. We mostly sell ready-knits to the public here. Perhaps the shop through there will help you."

She watched me walk across the floor, her manner suggesting that I might be a spy of some kind and regretting that she hadn't asked me for an ID. Maybe she watched too many crime movies or the old prison-camp atmosphere had got through to her too.

The shop was a blaze of color, a paradise for people who liked to buy their very expensive knitwear straight off the rack and say proudly back home, "I bought this in Stormer, the very place where it is made."

Most of the displayed models were well beyond my means. I couldn't see myself—or Susie—ever paying three hundred pounds sterling for a sweater. Susie had found the crafty way around the problem: buy the yarn and a pattern and knit it yourself.

There were a few shelves containing yarn and my luck was in. A large wire basket contained sales items, colors now of stock. And there was Susie's, the same batch number. I seized the hanks with a cry of triumph. As I paid for them, this bargain lot still seemed to cost a small fortune. I was glad that Laverock knitting fever hadn't affected me.

As the saleslady handed me the elegant and expensive bag marked with their trade name, I was aware of being watched. I turned quickly and caught a glimpse of the sun-hatted woman who moved quickly out of sight, but she gave me an idea.

I went back to the girl at reception, said how pleased I was with my purchase. I decided to resume a role I had once played before that saved my father wrongly accused of murder from a life sentence behind bars. I asked, "Would it be possible for me to have a word with Mrs. Laverock?"

The girl stiffened as if I had the temerity to ask to speak to royalty.

"I'm a freelance reporter for an Edinburgh newspaper. I would like to write a piece on Laverock Knitwear—good publicity," I added as her sour expression didn't change.

"You are a friend of Mrs. Laverock?"

I could hardly get away with that, so I said truthfully, "Someone pointed her out to me in the village this morning. When I saw her in the shop, I thought this would be a good opportunity—"

"Mrs. Laverock never gives press interviews. Never. Not to anyone. Good-day, miss."

And turning away she consulted the computer on her desk as if I had ceased to exist. I went out feeling crushed but happy that at least one reason for my visit had been successful. Susie would be delighted with her new yarn.

Now there was nothing to stop me from going back to Calum. Nothing but the climb back up the hill where I could get a bus on the main road. Nothing, that is, but Danny and seeing him tonight. And that, I was not going to miss. So I put aside all feelings of guilt and thought about how to fill in the hours before six o'clock.

I decided to buy a pack of sandwiches and some Coke at the general store and have a picnic down by the shore. It would be pleasant relaxing among the rocks in the sunshine and would give me plenty of time to sort out my thoughts.

As I left the shop, the sun shining straight in my eyes almost blinded me. A man almost collided with me. "Danny—what are you—? Oh, sorry!" It was his look-alike again.

I smiled apologetically. "I thought you were someone else." I began to walk away. He followed me.

"Excuse, miss. I hear you say Danny. You know Danny Lucas?" When I said yes, he went on, "You are a friend of his?"

"Yes."

"You tell me where to find him? I am friend also."

"Well, he has a van on the other side of the village.

Over there—" I gave him directions and then asked, "Have you tried the hotel? He works there sometimes."

"He not there. But I find him, thank you."

As he walked away I thought he looked as if he could be closely related to Danny. Same height, same coloring. It was a quite extraordinary likeness except that this fellow sounded foreign.

I think I was beginning to realize that what I knew of Danny was just the tip of an iceberg. There was a lot more to him that I didn't know and that I probably never would.

Danny was another puzzle to be left unsolved like the mystery of my missing mother. I had learned a lot about her early days from Dr. Brackley, hopefully enough to cure the nightmares that had haunted my life. I now knew the source of them, how as a small child I had witnessed an attempted murder and had been terrified out of my wits.

I had deliberately blocked out that whole scene and I knew now why my father wouldn't discuss it with me. I should be grateful since I'm sure he did it out of love for me. For my own good, he did not want that terrible day to rise to the surface of my memory again. It was safer for me if I believed her to be dead. And all the evidence said sadly that she was, that she and her lover had sunk to the bottom of the sea.

"Rest in peace, Mummy. I can forgive you for loving too well."

Although I loved Calum and wanted to spend the rest of my life with him, I also knew, to be perfectly honest with myself, that I had never yet met the love I would die for. And if Fate were kind, I never would.

So tomorrow I was going back to Calum forever. Tomorrow.

But it didn't happen like that. Murder was to be done before we met again.

CHAPTER 11

Sense told me that I should check with the hotel, see if Calum had left Airdbenn and if so, I should leave Stormer and head straight for Oban. I knew that I should go without delay, without waiting all day to spend the evening with Danny.

Sense told me I was sitting outside the lion's den waiting for the door to open, when I should be shaking the dust of Stormer off my heels.

I'd got Susie's yarn and she would be delighted. And from where I stood there was nothing else keeping me here. The time had come for me to face facts, that I was never going to find out what had happened to my mother. Dr. Brackley's story had simply added more mystery and confusion. I must content myself with the truth that my mother hadn't loved my father when she married him. She had come back to Stormer and gone off with the man she had wanted all her life and who wanted her.

It was a great romance—one I would have sighed over if it had belonged to someone else and I had not been the child she had abandoned. I'd always been brought up by Dad to understand that survival of the species was the mainspring of all life, and that the law of the universe was to produce babies and protect them so that they in turn could carry on the line.

If that was what fate intended, where did the great lovers fit in? Did they ever spare a thought about the survival of their offspring when they sailed off into the sunset together? Someday I must talk to my father about that after our cozy chat when I told him, as I intended to, what I had discovered in Stormer.

Such were my thoughts as I walked along the village street past the telephone booth. It was empty and I decided to call the hotel where I had left Calum.

The phone rang for some time before anyone picked it up. They would call Mr. Crail's room. I waited and put in more money. At last the voice said, "Sorry, there's no reply."

"Has he left?" I asked.

"One moment, please." Another wait, more coins in the box.

The voice returned. "Sorry to keep you waiting, but we seem to have problems with the computer this morning. There's been a big storm, it affects us that way—"

"Have you no other means of finding out if a guest has checked out?" I asked shortly. "What happened to good old guest registers and receipts?"

"Sorry—if you'll call back in a couple of hours, we're hoping to have the computer working again by then," she added hopefully.

I didn't share her optimism. "This is rather urgent.

When I left, Mr. Crail was feeling rather ill. I'd like to know if he has recovered. Couldn't you send someone up to his room to see?"

"One moment." A pause, a mutter of angry voices. "Sorry, I have a guest with an urgent problem to deal with and I cannot leave reception. Can I call you back?"

"No. I'm in a phone booth."

"Then if you'll try again later, I'll try and get your information."

An angry buzz as my money ran out. A tap on the glass, and a woman with a toddler by the hand smiled at me and mouthed that she needed the phone urgently.

I came out apologizing and went into the general store where I bought a sandwich and Coke and changed a note into coins to call Oban and leave a message for Calum's family. The woman had vacated the telephone booth but to my dismay, it had been taken over by a young lad, cigarette in hand, who was looking very relaxed and pleased with himself. The pile of coins beside him indicated he was chatting to someone special, probably his girl, and that he would be there for some time.

Oban, the hotel, and Calum would have to wait until later. From where I stood I had a good view of the Laverock factory at the east end and on the heights of the cliff face, Stormer Hall. Far below it lay the ruined church and the graveyard.

Well, there wasn't a great deal of choice, but I could explore all the sights of the village in a couple of hours. Meanwhile, I could find someplace to eat my lunch and call Calum later.

I headed for the ruin of Stormer Hall and found my way barred by locked gates. Such things didn't bother me. I went around the walls until I found a foothold on some stones and looked over into a bed of nettles at the side of the building.

It certainly looked grim, even on a day that was turning hot as well as sunny, but I wasn't put off. Protected from stings by my jeans and tennis shoes, I leaped over and made my way by an overgrown path to the front of the house.

Once there had been a terrace with steps down into a carefully tended formal garden. All that remained was a trail of destruction with some broken statues of dolphins amid the tangled shrubbery. Here and there a rose appeared, making a desperate bid for life while being strangled by the creeping weeds.

I sat on the steps and ate my lunch with what I guessed had once been a million-dollar view from the windows behind me.

As I got up to walk on, I saw a white face staring up at me through the grass. I leaped back. For a moment I thought I was looking at a skull, but then I saw it was just the head of poor old Neptune, his trident broken beside him. The rest of his body seemed to have vanished, an undignified end for a sea-god.

I looked up at broken windows, at trees growing through walls. It wasn't hard to believe that the house had been cursed. There was a heavy silence about the place, no birds chirping or singing, no sounds of any kind of life, only that ever-present beat of the triumphant, vengeful sea.

I was halfway down the stone steps when I heard a noise from inside the house. It was loud and unexpected, rather as if something heavy had been dropped, and the sound had echoed. It was enough to send a shower of rooks who had been quietly roosting in one of the tall trees screeching into the sky.

It scared the living daylights out of me, especially

when I saw a face staring down at me from one of the windows. A living face this time but one with no wish to be seen, for it was swiftly withdrawn.

The movement and desire for secrecy suggested another curious traveler who had no business here either. Someone who had been lucky enough to find a way into that sad ruin and did not want to be disturbed. He or she must have watched me sitting on the steps eating my lunch.

Someone with legitimate business—a land surveyor or estate agent—would not have ducked out of sight but would have stepped forward and demanded to know what I was doing here, reminding me that I had ignored the "Strictly Private, Keep Out! Trespassers Will Be Prosecuted!" signs at the gates.

I decided on a hasty retreat, and from where I was standing I could see the ruined walls of the old church. I hoped there would be a quick way through the graveyard and back into the village.

I was unlucky. Once again I came up against a padlocked iron gate which had given the occupants of Stormer Hall access to the graveyard. It conjured up melancholy thoughts of them using this route from the house, carrying coffins down the steep stone steps through the formal gardens and into the burial ground.

Climbing over the gate with extreme care, I found myself in the kingdom of the dead. I made my way over the grassy mounds that hid the dead of many generations. Huge tombstones, the lettering worn away by time and weather, leaned at crazy angles beside armless angels and broken urns.

Beyond this scene of desolation, a more welcoming gate led to the cliff path through the modern burial ground. Here the grass had been mown like a neat lawn around tidy marble headstones where flowers and wreaths marked the last resting places of Stormer's more recently mourned dead.

Lining the path between the ancient and modern sections was a small line of crosses with dates between the years 1940–45. There were no names, and I guessed these were the burials of unknown enemy airmen and sailors who had perished during the Second World War, their bodies washed up on the shore.

Alongside two small graves was the headstone: "In Memorium: R. Volti, P. Bacchi: R.I.P. 1943." Were these the graves of the two Italian prisoners Martha had told me about who had been shot trying to escape after robbing the local houses?

A little further away was a family vault with iron railings and the name "Selks" above the door. I paused awhile before the last resting place of my mother's foster-family. Another vault said "Halloway of Stormer Hall" with the names of the owner who had died in a bombing raid on London and his two sons who had perished on active service.

I looked back at the house, grim and stark against the bright afternoon sky. It must have been beautiful once, a great mansion built with such high hopes of good life. Now it was dead too, like this graveyard. It was all very sad and I wanted to be with the living again.

As I walked quickly toward the gate leading out to the cliff path, the sun glinted on something blue and bright at my feet.

I bent down and picked it up. A tiny blue bulb, the kind used in old flash cameras.

I held it in my hand. How strange! Who on earth would be wanting to take flash photos in the graveyard? I looked at the nearest headstone: "John Smithson, 1884–1943." How very odd! I wondered who this local worthy was that someone wanted to take a picture of his very ordinary grave.

Well, well, here was another minor mystery which need not concern me. Opening the gate, I set foot on the cliff path once again. Far below me were the sheer cliffs whose bases had been worn away by the breakers into tunnels and caves where seabirds nested.

An exciting place to explore, preferably by boat. On foot you would be in constant danger of being cut off by the incoming sea. As the tide was far out, I scrambled down by a narrow path used by sheep and at last stood on the stretch of golden sand beyond the pebbled shore. It looked warm and inviting.

Someone else had the same idea. I almost stumbled across a sunbather hidden by a large rock. I caught a glimpse of bare torso and bare legs stretched out before him. He was obviously fast asleep, enjoying a nap with a sheet of newspaper over his head to protect it from the sun.

A short distance away another figure, easily identified as Mrs. Laverock by the large sun hat, moved swiftly over the rocks, pausing to search the ebb-tide pools for seaweed to put in her basket over her arm.

This was my big chance. I decided to follow her, tell her how much we loved her knitwear in Edinburgh. She could hardly resist such flattery from a fan, or so I told myself.

However, she knew the terrain better than I did and by the time I had scrambled over the rocks and reached the spot where I first saw her, she was already halfway up the cliff path leading to the building at the far end of the village.

Too bad, I thought, but the sun was hot on my face and the warm, smooth sand begged me to relax for a while. I found a sheltering rock and removed my shoes, my socks, and my jacket, wishing I had a sun hat or a newspaper to cover my face like the sunbather. I decided to close my eyes and enjoy a few moments' rest.

I could have sworn that I wasn't asleep but a noise near at hand awakened me, a car backfiring, I thought. It was loud enough to upset the seabirds nesting in the cliffs and send them whirling into the sky in a screeching cloud of protest.

I sat up. I must have dozed, which was not surprising considering the events of the last twenty-four hours. My watch said that it was nearly five o'clock. I had rested much longer than I had intended and then a happy thought—

In an hour I would be seeing Danny again. I'd dash back to the manse, have a shower, change into my one dress, always carried in my backpack for practical purposes in case my jeans and T-shirt got soaked. Danny was sure to be impressed by this change from scruffy hitchhiker into some semblance of elegance.

It was as well I had wakened up too. The tide was coming in fast as I hurried back along the way I had come. To my surprise the sunbather was still there. He was just as I had seen him on the way down. He hadn't moved at all, legs stretched out before him, still sound asleep.

I wasn't sure what to do since he didn't realize the danger he was in. Perhaps he didn't know about the incoming tide. I had better warn him, although I felt a little embarrassed at doing so.

As I walked toward him, a sudden breeze caught the newspaper that had been shading his face and blew it across the sand. The sleeper was Danny.

Danny! I ran closer. His profile was toward me, his head lolling to the side. "Danny!" I said, but he didn't hear me. He was dead, a bullethole in his temple.

CHAPTER 12

"Danny! Danny!"

I ran to him, sobbing his name. Danny was dead.

And then I stopped. Close to him now, I could see through the blood streaking one side of his face that the dead man was Danny's look-alike.

Shocked and horrified as I was, all I could think of was to thank God it wasn't Danny.

I looked around, trying to keep calm, wanting to call for help, but the cliff path far above me was deserted. The tide was now coming in fast. Another half hour and the body lying by that large rock would be carried out to sea under the huge waves that swept in from the Atlantic Ocean.

I guessed now that he was probably already dead when I had stumbled across him on my way down to the shore.

I doubted if Mrs. Laverock had been aware that there was a dead man on the beach as she gathered her seaweed. I stood up, wondering what to do next. I knew from Calum's account of police procedure that I must not touch anything at the scene of crime.

The newspaper over his head had been a clever trick to keep away passersby, if there were any on that deserted shore. If this was suicide, there should be a gun. There was none. He had been murdered.

I glanced over my shoulder beyond the rocks to the dark shadows near the caves at the base of the cliffs. A sudden prickling sensation in the back of my neck told me that I was being watched. I froze. There might be a maniac at large in Stormer, and I was alone on the shore with a dead man at my feet.

Remembering how narrowly I had escaped death on the cliff path yesterday morning, I realized I had to get away from here as fast as possible and not tempt the killer with the prospect of a second victim.

If only I had a camera or even a piece of paper, I could at least make some record of the dreadful scene. And then I saw the newspaper that had covered his head, lying against a rock. That would do. I picked it up gingerly. Strangely enough there was no blood. I had a lipstick and quickly sketched the way the body lay against the rocks and the cliffs in the background. I had to admit it was very crude—a five-year-old could have made a better effort—but I folded it carefully and put it in the pocket of my jacket.

There was nothing more I could do but leave this terrible scene. As I ran, a sudden breeze blew a piece of white cardboard across my path. As it lodged face upwards against a rock, I saw that it was a faded black-and-white photograph of a man in uniform leaning against a gravestone, obviously taken long ago.

How curious, I thought. It must have been carried by the wind from some trash can in the village. On an impulse I thrust it into my pocket and forgot all about it in the drama of the next few hours.

As I looked back, I knew I had to find someone before it was too late. The killer had been clever when he lured his victim to the shore, its sheltering rocks the perfect place to leave an almost naked corpse. I wondered what had become of the dead man's clothes. Were they hidden somewhere nearby? The killer had thought it out very carefully, aware that with luck and those roaring breakers from the sea on his side, all evidence of his crime would be washed away forever. With even better luck, the murdered man might never be found at all.

Lost forever. Like my poor mother and her lover.

As I stumbled back up to the cliff path, I knew I must find Danny. He would know exactly what to do, I thought, as I headed for his van.

It was empty and locked. I stood there wondering where to go next. The only people I knew in Stormer were Martha MacVae and Jetta. One had a bad heart, and the other was lame. The news of a murdered man down on the shore would not be the best possible news for either of them.

There was no policeman in Stormer. Dr. Brackley had told me proudly—the citizens had their own rules of dealing with lawbreakers, treating them as he quaintly described it as "family affairs."

How had they accounted for those unknown corpses of enemy airmen and sailors washed up by the tides of war before being laid to rest under the row of white crosses in the churchyard? And how would a murder victim fit into this scenario?

But Dr. Brackley was Stormer's most senior citizen, and standing on the cliff top outside Danny's van, I was halfway to his cottage.

I ran all the way and arrived breathless. Praying that he was at home, I rushed in without knocking and called, "Dr. Brackley!" He came out of the sitting room looking dazed and half-asleep, still holding a newspaper as if he had been enjoying an afternoon nap.

"Please come—at once—there's a dead man lying on the shore!"

Dr. Brackley blinked several times, looking at me as if I had taken leave of my senses. Cupping his ear with one hand he repeated slowly, "A dead man, did you say?"

"Yes, yes. Please come quickly."

"If he's dead, then he won't go far away. How do you know he's dead?"

"He's been shot through the head."

The doctor stared at me openmouthed.

Then with a surprising turn of speed he grabbed his cane and an ancient bag containing his medical instruments. What use he thought they were going to be remained a mystery.

I was alarmed at his slow progress as I had to help him over the uneven patches down the cliff path. How on earth would he cope with a serious accident or someone bleeding to death? And this was murder!

At last we reached the rough path where I had climbed up from the shore. We were still in time, and I sighed with relief for the sea had not yet reached the rock where the dead man lay.

I pointed. "He's down there, lying behind that large rock."

The doctor peered down, leaning on his cane. "I don't see anyone, lass. Are you sure?"

"You can't see him from here. Wait until we get closer—I just left the place less than half an hour ago."

The doctor pursed his lips, eyeing the steep, uneven path down to the shore with dismay. The same thought was in my mind: How was he going to manage that?

I held out my hand. "I'll help you."

He sighed. "Right. But we'll need to take it very slowly."

As we went down, I watched the tide nervously as he leaned on me and I supported his weight at every step. Sometimes he stumbled and almost fell, taking me with him. We were going to lose this race against time and tide. At this rate we'd never reach the dead man before the tide, now moving in fast, covered him.

At last we made it and stood on the pebbled beach, getting our breaths back. I took my bearings on the scene. Yes, there were the steep cliffs I had drawn and closeby, the rock where the dead man lay.

"That's it!" I pointed again. "Over there, doctor." Even without my crude efforts at drawing, the scene was firmly fixed in my mind. It wasn't one I was likely to forget, ever!

There was only one difference. There was no body. Nothing!

"Where is he then?" the doctor demanded. "Are you sure this was the place?"

"Of course, I'm sure." I looked around. "I don't understand. He was lying here—dead, shot through the head." And then I knew what had happened.

"Someone must have moved the body—that's it!"

I heard the note of rising hysteria in my voice. Dr. Brackley never took his eyes off me, his manner like someone dealing with a mad patient who might turn nasty.

"You could be mistaken, lass. One rock looks very much like another," he sighed, deciding I was harmless after all. "Now then, you're sure it was on the shore you saw him?"

He pointed toward the steep black cliff face to our left. "There are lots of old caves there, very popular with the smugglers in the old days. Brandy for the parson and that sort of thing. Stormer has seen very exciting times."

"He was right here! I am positive about that, Doctor," I said firmly, in no mood for another lecture on folklore and legend.

"Well, well," he said.

But it wasn't well, well.

I looked past the rocks to the cliffs. "We could search your caves," I said. But the doctor didn't look very keen on that idea. I didn't fancy it much either, having to climb those steep, slippery rocks holding on to him.

I was saved the trouble, however, when he gave a little yelp and jumped back as an incoming wave touched his shoe. I knew it was too late now to search for the dead man, and the good doctor moved so slowly we would be in serious danger if we didn't get back right away to the safety of higher ground.

The rate at which he moved would be a problem in itself, but thankfully, it was easier for him climbing up than down. But by the time we stood breathless on the cliff path, the shore we had left was now covered by the sea. Huge waves were beating against the rock hiding the place where the dead man had lain, washing away all possible clues.

Dr. Brackley took my arm gently. "Come along, lass, and I'll make us both a nice cup of tea," he said in his best bedside manner.

Something in his manner made me feel foolish. He thought I had made the whole thing up. "There was a man there, I swear it. Wait a minute—I drew a picture of him."

I still had the newspaper in my pocket. As I unrolled it, even the doctor recoiled a little. "Is that blood?" he whispered.

"No, no. It's my lipstick—lips get dry, you know, in summer." That wasn't true; it was an excuse. I always carry a lipstick, my only makeup, and I feel undressed without it.

The doctor was frowning at my crude drawing of a man lying against a rock with a bullet wound in his temple. I guessed no one would ever take it seriously.

"I think I know who he was," I said. "I saw him in the village earlier today."

"What was he doing?"

"Just wandering around." I don't know why but at this stage I decided to keep to myself that he had been looking for Danny and I'd seen him talking to Mrs. Laverock.

I was aware that Dr. Brackley was watching me carefully again. "Tea?"

I looked at my watch. "Thank you, but I can't. I'm meeting someone at six." Danny, who was still gloriously, wonderfully alive.

"Then you'd better head back, hadn't you?"

"Yes." I turned to go. "What will you do?"

He looked at me. "What had you in mind, my dear?"

"You'll phone the police at Oban?"

"You just leave everything to me, I'll sort it all out. Off you go now and have a good time."

A good time, I thought. You must be joking.

He saw my hesitation, smiled broadly, and said, "Make the most of your stay in Stormer. It's full of history, you know."

And history as far as I was concerned was spelled d-a-n-g-e-r! My mother and her lover had drowned in an attempted murder by Jetta MacVae. I had hardly had time to set foot in Stormer before someone tried to kill me on the cliff path. And less than an hour ago, I'd found a dead man on the beach, shot through the head.

But how could I prove it? Dr. Brackley's manner suggested that he thought I was crazy. I guessed he had no intention of calling the police. He would go home and quietly forget the whole incident. After all, he had only my word for it, a stranger to Stormer, and no dead body as evidence!

He must have guessed that I was going to see Danny as I cut back across the cliff top, and I knew he was humoring me as he stood watching, leaning on his stick, as if I were a child he had to see safely across the road.

Danny would believe my story. I hadn't the least doubt about that! Danny would know what we should do!

CHAPTER 13

Danny was waiting for me. I was so glad to see him safe and unharmed that I had to restrain myself from rushing sobbing into his arms—a move which might have been misunderstood.

"How are you? What kind of day . . . ?" he asked.

I murmured vague replies, not knowing where to begin.

"Annie," he said as he took my arm firmly, "what's wrong?" He laughed. "No need to be nervous. Your virtue's quite safe, honest—I promise not to try to seduce you—at least," he added with a wicked twinkle in his eye, "at least not without your willing consent, that is." He paused and looked down into my face, suddenly serious. "However, if you're really unhappy about being here with me alone in the van, we can go down to the hotel—"

"Oh, no, Danny, it isn't that. It's nothing to do with you," I cried. "The most terrible thing has happened. You know that man I told you about—your look-alike? Well, I found him dead on the shore. He's been shot—"

And I gabbled out the whole story just as I had told
the doctor. Danny listened, occasionally throwing in
questions like cops ask: What time was that, what was he
wearing, did you see any weapon, and so on.

He took my arm. "Come on, what are we waiting for?
Show me—"

"I can't, Danny. When I went back with Dr. Brackley,
he—the dead man—had disappeared."

"Disappeared!" He gave me a hard look. "Are you
absolutely sure he was dead? I mean, you could have
been mistaken. He might have only been injured!"

"Come on, Danny. Injured? With a bullethole in his
head?"

He shrugged. "Doesn't sound very promising. Was
there anyone else on the shore who might have noticed
him?"

"Only Mrs. Laverock. She was out with her basket,
gathering seaweed at the rock pools, but she was at the
other end of the beach. I guess he would have been out
of her range of vision behind that rock."

He thought about that. "And she would come down
from the path near the ferry landing, the place they use
for transporting their goods from the factory."

"Well, even if she did see him, Danny, she probably
gave an almost naked man sunbathing a wide berth,
just as I did."

He nodded. "True enough. Who else have you told
besides Dr. Brackley?"

"No one. I came up here first hoping to find you—
especially as you move a lot faster than the doctor. He
didn't believe me—I'm sure he thought I was mad,

imagining a dead man on a beach whose body had disappeared."

"Hang on! Dead men can't get up and walk away. If you saw him, then he must still be there somewhere. Don't you understand, whoever shot him must have hidden his body when you went for help."

I shivered suddenly, remembering the feeling I had of being watched from the rocks. By a killer with a gun. "What are we to do?" I asked desperately.

Danny put his hand over mine. "We'll think of something," he said cheerfully.

"You do believe me, don't you?" I pleaded. It had never even crossed my mind that he might not.

"Yes, of course." But there was a hesitant note in his voice.

"We must tell the police, Danny."

"There isn't a resident cop in Stormer. I gather there never has been, according to Dr. Brackley. But anything major—like suicide or murder—would be dealt with by the Oban police. The doctor knows that."

"Danny," I interrupted, "a man has been murdered. We can't rely on the doctor. He thought I was imagining things. And I'd like to bet that he hasn't done a thing about it. We must phone the police ourselves—"

"Hold on, Annie." He looked at me sternly. "Think about it. We haven't much of a case to offer if there isn't a body."

"Come with me. I can show you where he was," I said desperately.

Danny shook his head. "Not much point to that, is there, Annie?" He avoided my eyes.

So he was having doubts about my story too. I felt sick and angry. "Danny, why on earth should I pretend all this happened if it didn't? I don't go around seeing corpses on beaches."

As he started to interrupt, I shouted at him, "Where's the point of making up such a story? Come on, you give me the reason!"

"All right, Annie. So there was a body and you saw it, but now it's high tide and it might never be seen again—the seas around here are pretty fierce."

And letting that sink in for a moment, he added, "So where is our evidence?"

"Here!" And once again I took the folded piece of newspaper out of my pocket.

Danny winced just like the doctor had at my crude drawing, as I explained that it was lipstick, not blood. Being folded up again hadn't improved its appearance. Badly smudged, it would be even harder for anyone to take this seriously as the drawing of a dead man lying against a rock with a bullet in his head.

Looking at it over Danny's shoulder, I noticed for the first time that this was the center spread of Stormer's free weekly newspaper.

"This could mean that the killer lives here."

"He could have picked it off a trash can. It would have been better if you'd handled it with gloves, Annie. The police might have been able to take fingerprints." He was silent, staring out of the window thoughtfully for a moment. There is something you should consider in all this, Annie."

He seemed reluctant to continue, so I said, "Right, let's have it then."

He regarded me solemnly. "First of all, I do believe you. Let's get that straight. I don't think you invented this story." Watching my face, he took my hand and held it tightly—a consoling gesture.

"Your reason for coming here was to find your mother. So let's agree that you came to Stormer in a highly emotional state after living for years with the obsession of not knowing what had happened to her."

He paused, shook his head, and added, "Let's face it. You came with one hell of a guilt complex, blaming yourself, thinking—rightly or wrongly—that she had some link with Stormer."

"Wait a minute! I don't think—I *know* she had. I had all the evidence I needed from Dr. Brackley's story. Don't try to tell me that was mere chance—my mother being called Bridie Ann too."

Danny held up his hand. "OK. Let me go on. You decide to find the truth once and for all, settle those old nightmares. You believe her death is a great mystery and that for their own reasons, the people here are trying to stop you finding out the truth."

"That's not true—I never said that!"

"Oh, I think it is true, Annie. I think you're ready to believe that Stormer is full of enemies. After all, you were sure this morning that someone tried to kill you on the cliff path."

"I didn't imagine that!"

He smiled. "Think about it, Annie. I worked that one out even as you were telling me the story. You imagined that a rock had been hurled down at your head. And that the sheep innocently grazing on the cliff above you—who were responsible for dislodging it—were really someone who meant to get rid of you."

I listened in stunned silence and when he paused for breath, I said, "I have another theory, Danny, one which I think you should consider very carefully."

"And what might that be?"

"The dead man—this stranger to Stormer—was the same guy who was asking for you."

"What makes you think that?"

"Well, I met him as I was leaving the Laverock factory. At first glance with the sun behind him, he could have been you, Danny. I thought you'd followed me, and then he asked if I knew where he could find you."

That got through to him. "When was this?" he asked sharply.

"After I left you. He was wandering about at the other end of the village."

"Did he say who he was?"

"No. Only that he was a friend. He sounded foreign."

"Foreign?" Danny frowned. Staring out of the window, he looked toward the sea as if there might be an answer out there.

He shook his head. "I haven't any foreign friends," he said bleakly.

"But surely the significance of all this isn't lost on you," I said.

Danny shrugged and I continued, "I think we've found a very good motive for our dead man."

"Such as?"

"Such as, you should be taking this as a warning."

"A warning? What kind of a warning?" He gave a puzzled laugh. "Sorry, Annie, you've lost me."

"Then you're not as sharp as I thought you were. I think it's fairly obvious that whoever killed that man made a mistake."

"What kind of mistake?"

"Whoever killed that poor guy thought it was you!"

Danny stared at me and laughed out loud. "Don't be daft, Annie. I'm a part-time chef at the hotel. I hardly know anyone in Stormer except the MacVaes. Who would want to kill me, for heaven's sake?"

I smiled. "Precisely, Danny. You're now repeating my words almost exactly."

"I don't understand."

"We both want to know who has tried to kill us, and for what reason."

Danny sprang up from his chair. "Look, Annie, this is crazy nonsense," he said angrily.

That was too much. I got up and seized my jacket. "If that's the way you feel, Danny, I'd better be on my way. Thanks for listening."

At the door he grabbed me by the arms and turned me to face him. "Annie—oh Annie," he said softly. "I didn't mean that—honest."

He kissed me for the first time. And it was so good—it was what I needed at that moment—warm, comforting arms to hold me. A moment later he released me and whispered, "Friends, eh, Annie? Let's be friends, how about that? Drown the whole grisly story with a pizza and a bottle of wine."

I smiled. If there were more kisses like that on the menu and this was just the starter course—wow! So I tried my best, laughed at his jokes, and listened to the latest pop record on his CD. As if that weren't enough to win my heart, the pizza, which he had made himself, was the best ever, and the salad was good too. And the wine—I thought I really ought to stop him from opening that second bottle, but I didn't.

I got a bit giggly after that. I told him all about the

little black dress and how I had been hoping to impress him that I wasn't always a scruffy hitchhiker. I let him kiss me again. My head was whirling, my body responding to his caresses.

"I never thought you were anything but very special, Annie."

"You're joking."

"No, I'm not. You have the most gorgeous eyes and I seem to remember those great legs that went on forever in that short skirt."

"Honestly?" Flattered, I giggled again.

"Honestly. Pity we have to have them covered by jeans most of the time." His hands were on the waist, the zip. "Let's change all that, shall we?"

Through the mists of wine, I surfaced for a moment. "No, Danny—I don't think we should."

"Why not?" he whispered. "You're very special to me. I knew that from the first time when I saw you at that wedding."

That wedding! Danny trying to get me into bed had said exactly the wrong words. They jolted me back to the real world, the world beyond Stormer that still existed and waited for me. The world I belonged to with Calum.

He felt the change in me, that I was no longer responding. "What's wrong now?" He let me go and he sounded angry.

"Everything's wrong, Danny. No, not with you—with me. I'm going."

He stood with his back to the door, barring my exit.

"Please, Danny, let me go."

He lunged forward to kiss me again, and over his

shoulder I saw the blank wall, the pieces of tape that were still there, the faint marks of photos and posters removed in a hurry of the girls who had gone before me in—I hadn't the least doubt—the same evening ritual. Superb cooking, too much wine. Even a poor chef could have thought up that one and Danny was ace, the very best in his field.

I turned my face away. He took my chin in a firm hand, forced his lips on mine, his body pressing me against the door.

I panicked then. I didn't really want to struggle with him, to fight for what little virtue I had left. But the dangerous moment had passed. His deep sigh said that it was too bad, but he didn't usually have to fight for what he wanted. His glance was mocking. "Go, then, Annie—to your lonely bed, see if I care!"

Smiling, he opened the door. "Don't think too badly of me—I thought it was what you wanted too. We both had a lot of wine and I got the signals all wrong. Sorry." He held out his hand. "No hard feelings, Annie?"

"Of course not, Danny." I was so glad he felt like that.

"Wait and I'll walk you home," he called after me.

But I was already halfway down the path, a little unsteady perhaps but feeling very virtuous indeed. And more than a little confused. Something more than a guilty conscience was bothering me in Danny's van.

Once my head cleared, I would try to remember what it was.

CHAPTER 14

The bracing wind got rid of most of the effects of Danny's wine and I knew I wouldn't sleep, so I went on down to the village street and called Calum in Oban.

It was the Irish cousin who picked up the phone. There was a lot of noise in the background, mostly female, and I had to repeat my name twice before she realized who I was. I heard a voice beside her whisper "Who is it? Oh, I'll talk to her. Hello, Annie darlin', it's me." (Me being Calum's mum.) "Sure now, Calum's off to the pub with the boys, just havin' a few jars—"

I'd thought Calum would have had enough of the drink to last him a long time. Had he recovered?

"He's just great, Annie—and he's longing to set eyes on you again—we all are. Sorry about the noise—the girls are having a bit of a hen party. Shut up, will you?"

That fell on deaf ears and she came back to me. "Can

he call you back when he comes in?"

I said the manse where I was staying didn't have a phone, but I'd call him in the morning. Then my coins ran out.

For a while I stood looking over the sea, breathing in the pure air. There was a moon and the waves glistened like silver as I walked swiftly up the path to the manse.

I needed space to think, to clear my mind regarding the day's events. And I had to confess that the major problem to sort out was no longer the disappearing dead man on the shore but the very much alive Danny I had just left. To be honest I was feeling bad at having walked out on him like a foolish virgin and very much afraid that we might not meet again before Calum arrived to collect me. I hadn't any doubt that he would come for me, but to be on the safe side, I'd find out what time the Oban bus passed the top road where the Airdbenn wedding party had set me down.

I slept soundly with one weird dream about Danny and the dead man, but it faded the moment I opened my eyes.

At breakfast next morning in response to Martha's questions about how long I'd need the room, I said, "My fiancé's coming to collect me—"

"Your fiancé? You're engaged to be married?" She looked surprised and a little shocked.

"Yes, I am."

"Well, now." She gave me a hard look. "I thought you were Danny's girlfriend."

"No," I said firmly and with a twinge of regret. Maybe he didn't bring girls here after all and I was special as he had told me last night. Too late now, Danny, I thought as I went to the telephone booth.

This time it was Calum who picked up the phone. He started to tell me how much he was missing me

112 Alanna Knight

and so forth. Had my little trip to Stormer been worth all the trouble?

"You've been missing a terrific time," he said. "The Belfast cousins are great—they have a band. You should see us all doing Irish dancing."

My coins were running out so I said, "Can you come for me right away?"

There was a slight pause. "That's a bit difficult. I've promised to take Sean and Mum—"

The coin-box gave a warning click. "Check the buses, Annie, there must be buses to Oban. Find out and let me know—I'll meet you." Another click and that was that. He was gone.

I decided the hotel would have a bus timetable. However, a notice on the door said "Open at 11 A.M." I walked away feeling that the whole world was against me. The real reason was that I felt badly let down. What made it so hard for Calum to drop everything, tell Sean and his mother that I needed him, and come to Stormer right away?

In the general store the checkout girl shook her head. "Bus timetables? I'm sorry we don't have any. Most folk have their own cars. You could try the hotel."

She didn't sound very hopeful. Thanking her, I saw that Mrs. Laverock was behind me. Her garb didn't look so strange this morning with the sun shining in what promised to be a hot summer's day.

"Excuse me." Mrs. Laverock had followed me out. She smiled as she said, "I heard you asking about buses to Oban. I can't tell you offhand, but we do have some timetables in the office if you'd like to come with me."

"Thank you very much."

As we walked, we exchanged the usual remarks about

the weather and it being a better day. She asked how long I was staying and I said I was leaving today.

"Is this your first visit?" she asked.

I said it was and she hoped I would come again. "You were one of the main reasons for my visit," I said.

"I was?" She laughed. "Of course. You were in the shop buying yarn. Are you a keen knitter?"

"No, it's for one of my friends—she needed some colors matching."

"Oh, do you live nearby?" She smiled. "You don't sound as if you come from these parts."

"Actually I'm from Edinburgh," I said.

She laughed. "That's a long way to come for yarn for a friend. You must be a very kind person."

We reached the factory and she led the way to the reception desk and waited while the girl searched for bus schedules to Oban.

"Mondays, Wednesdays, and Saturdays—that's all. Morning and evening. You could get one this evening about seven from the top of the road."

"That's super."

Mrs. Laverock had waited with me. "Why don't you call your friends from here? Morag will get the number for you."

Calum's Irish cousin Maeve answered. "They're all away to play golf, Annie, but I'll tell Calum about the bus. I think they're having lunch at the club. The bus gets in—what time did you say?"

Calum was having the life of Riley. He'd never believe my story of danger and disappointment, either.

"Get through all right?" Mrs. Laverock asked. I thanked

her for her help and she smiled. "Would you like a coffee while you're here?"

I followed her into a refreshment room furnished with the same taste and expense that marked Laverock Knitwear as she said, "Do sit down. I'll get it."

The waitress came with two coffees, and Mrs. Laverock took a seat opposite. "Well, you have come a long way—Edinburgh's on the other side of the country. Have you lived there long?"

"All my life, ever since I can remember. My father is from the Highlands—he has a bookshop in the Royal Mile."

"Really! How interesting. I love to read, but I have so little time these days."

We talked about books and how she liked biographies and historical novels. Then we had a second cup of coffee while she told me about the natural processes of dyeing wool.

"I've noticed you out on the shore gathering seaweed."

"That's right. You have to be very careful about the tides. I'm apt to wander when I'm looking for something quite special. Once or twice I've almost had to swim back—and that isn't easy—the tides are fast and very dangerous."

I agreed and said I'd taken a nap yesterday afternoon in the warm sunshine.

"That was very risky!" She sounded alarmed as she added, "I didn't notice you or I'd have warned you."

What about the sunbather? But somehow I couldn't bring myself to spoil the good impression I was making by asking if she had happened to see a dead man lying beside a rock or happened to hear a gun shot.

"Have you lived here long?" I asked.

She smiled. "A very long time." She looked at me. "Since I was quite young, about your age." She sounded sad and, removing her glasses, she rubbed her eyes gently.

When she turned to look at me, I saw that they were brilliant blue and that in those far-off days when she first came to Stormer, she must have been a lovely young woman. She must have seen my surprised expression and she said, "I have a skin problem, and I have to keep covered up. A few years ago I developed skin cancer. It was very unpleasant so now I stay clear of the sunshine. But when I am forced to spend so much time at the shore, I am apt to forget what the weather is like. I stay out too long and even when there is a wind blowing and it seems cool, I forget that the sun rays can still be dangerous."

I looked at her as she talked, a nice, warm woman. I wondered how I had ever thought there was something sinister about her because I am good at picking up vibrations; I guessed that she was sad and lonely despite her success. I doubted whether there was a Mr. Laverock and suspected that she was either a widow or divorced.

"What takes you to Oban?" she asked. "Is it more yarn for this lucky friend of yours?" she added with a laugh.

"No, that side of my visit is finished. I'm off to meet my fiancé." And soon I was telling her about Calum, about his being a detective sergeant in the Edinburgh City Police and how we were getting married soon.

She sighed. "How lovely. Such an exciting time in one's life." She looked very sad as she added, "I've been on my own now for more years than I care to remember."

So I had been right!

"Mrs. Laverock." It was the girl from reception. "There's a call coming through for you. It's from Chicago."

She stood up. "Oh, I must go—finish your coffee. And

do excuse me—it's been so nice talking to you." Turning to go, she said, "I don't even know your name."

"It's Ann—Bridie Ann."

She went white, and for a moment, I thought she was going to faint. Her lips moved. "Bridie Ann," she whispered.

"They're waiting, Mrs. Laverock. I've put it through to your office," said the girl.

With one final horrified glance at me, she turned quickly and was gone.

CHAPTER
15

I left the Laverock factory premises feeling as if I had two heads, like some kind of an alien monster. Two women in Stormer had almost fainted when I mentioned my name, so what was it about Bridie Ann that terrified the wits out of both of them?

Dr. Brackley's account of the early days of the woman I believed to be my mother had made me understand Jetta's reactions. After all, my mother had gone off with Jetta's husband. But Mrs. Laverock? Where did she fit into the scenario? Had she known my mother too?

"Annie!"

Deep in thought, I almost walked past Danny coming out of the general store staggering under the weight of a large box of groceries.

"Annie, hi! Where are you off to? I thought you'd gone to Oban."

"I am going—later today."

He looked at me sadly. "Back to the best man, eh? So I'm going to lose you after all."

"'Fraid so," I said lightly, trying to sound as if I didn't care in the least.

"When do you go?"

"There's a bus to Oban that goes past the road end at seven—"

"I can save you that ordeal, Annie. To be honest, bus timetables aren't strictly kept in this part of the world." He put down the box. "Look, I have a gig just outside Oban tomorrow night. How about that? I can guarantee to deliver you safely into the arms of your man if you don't mind riding on the bike again."

When I hesitated, he put a hand on my arm and whispered, "Please, Annie. It'll give us one more day before we part forever, as the song goes."

My mind was racing ahead. Another twenty-four hours in Stormer and I might solve the mystery of the disappearing dead man, murdered because he looked like Danny. It was a challenge I was unable to resist— especially as no one, not even Danny, believed my story and I was determined to prove that I was right! So I accepted his offer.

"You will? That's great!" He sounded so surprised and pleased that I was touched and flattered.

"I'll need to call the Oban folks and tell them," I said without a pang of conscience. Having to wait another day for my arrival would serve Calum jolly well right for being so unwilling to give up a terrific time with his Irish cousins to come to Stormer for me. The round-trip to Stormer and back to Oban by car would only take an hour! One hour! And that still smarted. If he loved me, then he would be ready to come when I needed him. My Edinburgh friends might laugh at such an old-fashioned idea, but that's the way I felt it should be between a man and woman who loved each other.

Danny was chatting about the gig in Oban, unaware that I hadn't heard a word. He nodded toward the hotel. "I have to get this food to the kitchen, prepare a few dishes for the freezer, and make up some menus for them." He grinned. "And collect some wages! Shouldn't take too long. Then I'm yours for the rest of the day—and night."

He saw the shadow on my face and added quickly, "Is there anything you'd like to do? The last chance to see the secret life of Stormer?"

I looked at him. "I'd like to explore the old caves, the ones the smugglers were supposed to use."

Danny was suddenly solemn. "You're still hoping to find your missing body, aren't you?

"Of course not." But even to myself I didn't sound very convincing.

"Come on, Annie. I can read your mind and I think you should give up any ideas in that direction."

There was no point in arguing with him and I didn't much like the way he referred to the dead man as "your missing body" as if it were one of my own inventions.

At that moment a woman came out of the telephone booth, my chance to escape.

"See you later," I said and dashed in to phone Oban. I had three one-pound coins which I hoped would be enough.

Thankfully Calum answered. "Annie, darling, how are you? It's great to hear your voice. God, I've missed you. Have you missed me? I'm longing to see you."

My heart melted at the warmth and tenderness in his voice. "I'm longing to see you too."

"Darling Annie—what time does the bus arrive? The family will wait supper—they're dying to meet you."

"Well, I hope they can survive another day without me."

"Another day?" He sounded shocked. "I thought you were coming this evening."

"I was, but I have the chance of a lift tomorrow. I've decided to accept it since I've been told the buses aren't very reliable—you can wait for ages—if the weather's bad—" I rattled on.

"All right, all right." But his deep sigh said it wasn't. "Who's bringing you to Oban? Someone with a good car, I hope?"

"I wouldn't be accepting otherwise, would I? And it's a motorbike actually. You know the fellow—you met at the wedding. Remember Danny?"

"Danny? No."

"He played the fiddle with the group. You said you thought he was great."

A small silence. "I didn't know that was his name. But Jim said he thought he fancied you. He'd seen him eyeing you from the band and he dashed across to ask you to dance while I was—er, away."

I could hear the cold chill in his voice all the way from Oban, the suspicion, but I wasn't going to deny it. "He's been a great help, a real friend in need," I said defensively. "When the minibus set me down at the crossroads—it's a three-mile hike down to Stormer, you know—he picked me up on his bike."

The silence deepened and I wondered if Calum had hung up. But I didn't care. A devil seized me as I went on, "I don't know what I would have done without Danny. He's not only a great fiddler, he's a super chef."

"Sounds as if you've been spending a lot of time with him." His voice told me he was making an effort to sound cool and relaxed about Danny, but he wasn't succeeding very well.

"Just the evenings. I get lonely. There's not much to do staying here in the manse—no TV, not even a phone— and no movies in the village—"

"Annie," he interrupted desperately, "why didn't you just wait another day at Airdbenn instead of rushing off on your own like that? I was fine by the next day and we could have gone to Stormer together—you didn't need to suffer all that hassle."

"Oh, I haven't been suffering in the least. I've really enjoyed being here—" (What a lie!) "—and Danny has promised to bring me right to your cousin's door. It's no trouble; it's on his way to the gig."

"Find out anything useful about your mother?"

"Not really, but I did find a dead man on the beach."

"You—what?"

"He'd been shot—we don't know who he was. Great drama—"

"Say that again."

I repeated it and he said, "Have the police been informed?"

"I expect so—" I could see the coins in the meter ticking away.

"Now, listen to me, Annie, you're not to get involved."

"I don't know what you mean."

"I know you, Annie!"

The coins ran out at that. Just in time, as I could feel another lecture coming on.

I wished I'd had time to say good-bye—and that I loved him. I did, but my feelings were all mixed up. I knew I had been mean, trying to make him jealous like that just for spite.

Now I felt sorry and guilty too that I couldn't resist the chance of going with Danny on the bike to Oban instead of being a virtuous, loyal fiancée and waiting for the bus that evening on the bleak main road above Stormer.

It would be several hours before I met Danny, and I knew I hadn't been kidding about those caves either. I couldn't get them out of my mind ever since the dead man disappeared. I had hoped I could get Danny to go with me. I didn't much fancy going alone, not knowing the tides and so forth.

A sudden bout of sneezing had me diving into my pocket for a tissue. My hand touched a piece of cardboard. In a panic rushing to find someone to tell about the dead man, I'd forgotten all about the photo I picked up on the cliff path. About to throw it in the trash can near the general store, I looked at it again.

How odd that someone should have had their picture taken leaning on a tombstone. The man's uniform suggested that it had been taken in wartime. He looked sad too. Was it some relative's grave? I was certain that the blurred outline of a wall behind him was the ruined church on the headland above Stormer I had walked past yesterday.

As I walked quickly along the cliff path, I noticed the seals gathered on the rocks far below, but they were silent. No doubt saving their energies for the evening performance. I felt excited as well as curious about the photograph I had discovered. Had it been lost by some member of the family while visiting the grave?

As I went through the iron gate leading into the modern burial ground, I realized there were so many marble slabs exactly like the one in the photograph, I didn't know where to begin.

"Good morning, Annie." It was Dr. Brackley, carrying a bunch of roses. Limping toward me, he looked very old and frail. "This is my day for putting flowers on Milly's grave. It's forty years ago this weekend that she died." He looked sad, almost tearful, poor old man. "She was a lovely woman, everyone loved her."

At least she'd never grew old in his eyes, I thought. She had never lived to see the carnage of old age on those we love. She lived forever in the land of eternal youth, cherished and kept alive by his memories.

"What are you doing here?" he asked.

"I found a photo yesterday—" and I showed it to him, telling him how I'd found it and thought it might belong to some relative.

As I talked, he held it in his hand and took out his glasses for a better look. "I know who this is, Annie. I recognize him."

"You do?" Here was a piece of luck.

"I do indeed. Its Paulo Volti, one of the two Italian prisoners of war who was shot trying to escape from the camp where the Laverock factory now stands."

He shook his head. "How extraordinary—you say you found it on the cliff path? I wonder how it got there. What were you going to do with it?"

"I don't know. I just thought I'd try to locate the headstone—it might give me some clues."

He laughed. "Clues, eh. A bit of a detective, are you?"

I smiled apologetically. "Not me, but my boyfriend is—

he's with the Edinburgh police. It's the sort of thing he would do. I wouldn't know where to start looking."

Dr. Brackley sighed. "I can't imagine how it got here. Someone from the village must have dropped it. May I have another look?"

I handed it to him and he took from his waistcoat pocket a small magnifying glass. "I need this these days for the small print," he said, studying it carefully. "There's faint letters, carved on the stone—you can just see them. Here take a look."

I could see them clearly though the glass. "John Smi—"

"John Smithson, that's it. He was the village blacksmith. Died just a few days before the Italians tried to escape. I remember it perfectly. I'd just been to the funeral—he was my Milly's uncle. Come with me, Annie."

We walked toward the row of crosses, the two Italian graves, and the headstone I had noticed on my first visit. We stood looking at it together as if it might provide us with the answer.

"I wonder what it all means, Annie. It's got me licked," said the doctor.

I had a sudden idea. "The man I told you about—the one I found dead on the beach—he was foreign, very dark and swarthy. Perhaps he was a relation of Paulo Volti and had come to Stormer to find his grave."

Dr. Brackley nodded. "Yes, that's very possible. A lot of Italians have come back through the years to pay homage to the men who were here in Stormer as prisoners of war. Fathers, brothers, cousins—they're very sentimental about such things. Some of them made friends with folks here who had been kind to them. They still keep in touch, bring their families to visit, take pictures and so forth."

That, I thought, accounted for the flashbulb I had found beside John Smithson's grave. While the doctor frowned over the photograph, rubbing his chin thoughtfully, I had another question for him. "Did you tell the police in Oban—about what happened yesterday?"

"Yesterday?" he repeated vaguely.

"Yes, about the murdered man I found on the shore," I explained patiently.

"Oh, yes," he turned to me. "Oh, yes. They said it was difficult when the body had disappeared, but to leave it with them, they'd consult their list of missing persons. That was the best they could do in the circumstances."

As he was talking, I could just imagine the scene in the Oban police office. Another daft old man, they'd be saying, hoaxed by some teenager. No big deal; it happened all the time. They'd record the call, of course, and that would be the end of it.

I put out my hand. I wanted the photo back. I no longer had any intention of throwing it away. It was evidence.

An alarming thought stirred at the back of my mind. I was almost certain now that the man who dropped the photo of Paulo Volti was the dead man, Danny's look-alike. Someone had followed him and killed him—by mistake.

I was right. It had been Danny they wanted!

CHAPTER 16

I was determined to find out what had happened to the dead man, who he was, and why he had disappeared. I can't imagine why I was convinced that I would succeed before I left for Oban with Danny the following evening. The weather was against me, for a start.

The rain began, and the horizons and the islands were lost from view. At such a dismal prospect even the seals were barking in melancholy protest, so I decided to retreat to my pleasant room in the manse. There I'd sit down comfortably with a sheet of paper before me and try to work it all out logically, using the rules of observation and deduction as my hero Sherlock Holmes would have done.

The hallway smelt damply of wet umbrellas and raincoats, but in the kitchen Martha and Jetta were making raspberry jam. It smelt delicious and I lingered for a while as they commented on the weather which they assured me kindly was just a passing phase.

"If it's really set in, the seals don't bark like that."

At last, saying I had cards to write, I headed upstairs and settled down to write a report on all the things I had seen connected with the dead man. Never to my dying day would I forget the shock of finding him, those few seconds of absolute horror when I thought he was Danny. And when I went closer, I had realized this was the same man who asked me about Danny when we met outside the Laverock factory.

I took from my backpack the folded sheet of newspaper with its lipsticked drawing of the death scene, now so badly smudged it was difficult to make out any of the details.

The likeness to Danny worried me. The dead man had said he was a friend, so there must be a definite connection. Could it be something Danny didn't know or was unaware of? I was certain that the vital clue lay in what Dr. Brackley had told me about the Italian prisoners of war when he had identified the man in the photograph as Paulo Volti, who was shot trying to escape from the camp that was now the site of Laverock Knitwear's factory.

The discovery of the photograph could not be dismissed as coincidence. What I held in my hands was a vital clue to the murder of the man I had found on the shore. All that was missing was a motive. According to Calum and detectives in charge of murder cases, the reasons were most usually connected with love, loathing, or lucre (i.e., money).

My mind raced ahead with a sudden surge of excitement. The link between the dead man and Paulo Volti's photo might well be the stolen hoard that he and his colleague Bacchi had hidden away.

But if the dead man had come back to find it, how did he connect with Danny, who looked so like him that the killer had shot the wrong man? What if they were related, long-lost cousins?

I dismissed that theory as too romantic. Danny Lucas, despite his exotic coloring, sounded very English and said he had no foreign friends. He had been as puzzled as I was by the man he had never met but who claimed to know him. I wondered if, in his fleeting visits to Stormer, Danny had been even remotely interested in the wartime drama of the Italian prisoners and the robberies at Stormer Hall and other houses.

We were about the same age, and it was always possible that some remote family link with Italy existed in his grandparents' generation that he knew nothing about.

I felt really excited about this new discovery. I hadn't time to wait until evening when we would meet again, so I decided to go down to the hotel on some excuse and try to have a word with him there.

I was about to leave when I heard voices in the hall and Martha called upstairs, "Annie! There's a gentleman here to see you. He's in the parlor."

Calum! For a moment I thought he had come for me after all! I ran downstairs, and it was Danny, of course.

"Hi, Annie. Will you come to the hotel for dinner at seven? I have to cook for some guests tonight, so I won't be able to get away."

He laughed. "It's your big chance to see for yourself the chef seriously at work."

But I was hardly listening. Food and Danny's superb cooking didn't seem of any importance at that moment. I was dying to tell him about the Italian connection.

"Danny," I said. "Tell me something about yourself."

He looked startled. "This is rather sudden. What would you like to know?"

"Oh, just the usual things, where were you born, how old you are."

He smiled. "The hard ones first, eh? I was born in London. I'm twenty-six and I've lived in Scotland since I left the university four years ago. I'm unmarried— still hoping."

"What about your parents?"

He looked sad. "I never knew them, Annie. They were both killed in a car crash in Spain when I was two years old—or at least that's what they told me at Dr. Barnardo's."

"Barnardo's! So you were brought up in an orphanage!" I said excitedly.

"Yeah—no big deal, but they were good to me." He shrugged. "I try to forget all my early life. It doesn't amount to very much but it's thanks to them that I got a good education and was able to make my way in the big, bad world. I learned to cook when I was old enough to be left alone in the kitchen with hot pans."

Aware of my excited expression as he was speaking, he paused and regarded me curiously. "Mind telling me what this is all about, Annie?"

"But that dead man—he knew you."

He sighed wearily. "How could he, Annie? We've been through all this before."

He sounded bored and slightly impatient and I said, "Then how did he know your name? He said he was a friend, and he was your double. And if you never saw him—how do you know you hadn't met somewhere? Perhaps in some hotel where you worked and he remembered you."

Danny shrugged. "That's one possibility, I suppose. But I think I'd have remembered a man who was my double."

"Well, whether you met or not, he knew of your existence and that you were in Stormer." I let that sink in. "I believe he had come to Stormer with some vital information to pass on to you, Danny. Of that I'm quite sure."

"Such as?"

"I don't know what, or I wouldn't be asking you. But from what you've told me about not knowing your parents and being brought up in an orphanage, perhaps he was going to tell you that you were long-lost cousins."

"That is too fantastic, Annie." And Danny laughed out loud.

"No, it isn't. I think I know who he was—the man who I found murdered—"

"And whose body mysteriously disappeared—" Danny said cynically.

I ignored that. "I'd be prepared to bet he was here on some vital errand."

"Such as? This had better be a good reason."

"Then let's just suppose that he was kin to the Italian prisoners of war," I interrupted.

"Hardly a good reason for someone killing him. The war was a long time ago."

"But there is a link with that past, a stolen hoard which was never recovered from robberies in the big houses, including Stormer Hall, where the Italians worked in the gardens."

Danny paused, looked at me as if I had taken leave of my senses, and then shook his head. "That is a wild idea, Annie. Hidden treasure and all that sort of thing. I guess you've been reading too many crime novels."

Pausing to let me digest that, he said, "And I still don't know what all this has to do with me. Where do I come into this fantasy of yours?"

"I'm coming to that. Just suppose that your grandfather, whom you don't know anything about, had been one of the Italian prisoners buried in the graveyard here."

"That's absurd!"

Ignoring his mocking laugh, I went on, "Don't you understand, Danny, it all fits. The first time I saw you, I thought your looks were a tad too exotic to be British. Anyone could mistake you for Italian."

My theory didn't impress Danny. He merely shrugged. "I've never given much thought to who I was and so forth. I just accepted that I was an unidentified Barnardo's orphan."

"Was Lucas your real name then?"

He shook his head. "I've no idea. You accept whatever you're given."

"What does it say on your birth certificate?"

"The one I had was a copy of the original—so they told me. It was very basic." With a shrug of impatience he went on, "So where is all this getting us, Annie? It's what I am now, what I've made of my life that's really important to me, and I've never been even mildly interested in tracing my roots."

Stubbornly I said, "I still think someone tried to kill you because of your roots, Danny."

"What?"

"The man who was shot was definitely looking for Danny Lucas. You hadn't met, you say, but he knew of you. He had tracked you down to this obscure part of

Scotland. He must have had some reason. So what was it? Did he only want to shake you by the hand and call you cousin? Or was it some more sinister reason?"

"A sinister reason?" Danny repeated with a laugh. "Now you have lost me, Annie."

"Think about vengeance—the Mafia—the blood feuds—"

"You're joking!"

"No, I'm not. You see, I have a theory."

Danny grinned. "Another one? This had better be good."

"Oh, it is. I believe that this man I talked to was Italian, and something or someone had brought him to Stormer. The photo I found on the cliff path belonged to him."

"Photo? What photo was this?"

I realized I hadn't told Danny about that, and when I pulled it out of my pocket, he frowned over it for a while before handing it back.

"From someone's family album—what's the significance?"

"I think it belonged to the killer or the dead man, and he dropped it on the way down to the shore," I said triumphantly.

"Let me have another look," Danny sounded interested for the first time.

I explained, "Dr. Brackley recognized it as Paulo Volti, who was shot trying to escape from the prison camp. What if the dead man was related to him?"

I paused and Danny smiled tolerantly. "I get it. You think he came back to collect the stolen goods they had salted away."

I shook my head. "Not entirely. It was mostly vengeance. He had the blood feud to avenge but hopefully he'd find the treasure to make his journey worthwhile. Kill two birds with one stone, so to speak."

"Go on—" Danny said mockingly.

"There were two Italians shot in the escape attempt. What if the dead man was in Stormer looking for the descendant of the man who had betrayed them to the prison guards and caused their deaths? The man whose name we don't know."

"And who you think might have been my unknown grandfather." Danny's laugh told me how far-fetched the idea was. "It doesn't get us much nearer to the hidden treasure, does it?" he added.

I shook my head. "As I've said, I don't believe that was his main object."

"So who shot him then? Any ideas?" I shook my head and he went on, "You've got a theory that whoever killed him thought it was me. Well, that just doesn't make sense unless he knew a lot more about my grandfather than I do."

"Or unless someone else in Stormer knew about both of you."

"That's impossible. I don't know anyone in Stormer. As I've told you, I'm a passing stranger. I help out in the hotel and the only other people I know are the MacVaes."

"Wait a moment, Danny. There is someone else. I saw him talking to Mrs. Laverock the first day I was here."

"Mrs. Laverock," said Danny slowly. "Perhaps you have something there, something neither of us have ever considered—the woman of mystery. No one seems to know much about her, do they?"

I shook my head. "Not even Dr. Brackley, and he's lived here for sixty years and knows all about everything and everyone." I paused. "When I was at the factory, she kindly gave me coffee—"

"She did? Then you must be among the privileged few."

"Not only that, she was prepared to be friendly. She told me she was a widow and had lived in Stormer for years and years."

My mind was racing ahead, trying to fit the pieces, as Danny interrupted, "But no one knows anything about her background either. How old would you say she is?"

"I'm hopeless at ages, but I'd guess fifty-ish."

"So she could have been born at the end of the war." Danny paused. I felt that he was interested at last as he went on, "She certainly looks a bit odd, wearing that sun hat and dark glasses on a rainy day. What if she had a very good reason for concealing her real identity?"

"You mean—?"

"Yes, Annie," said Danny. He sounded really excited for the first time, as if we were really on the verge of a discovery. "What if she is our missing link? What if she came to Stormer originally because she had a connection with the Italian prisoners? Perhaps she was the daughter of the informer and knows a whole heap more than any of us what went on. What if she lured the Italian fellow here?"

"And led him to the beach and then shot him! Danny, I think you might have something there."

"Don't you remember, Annie? You told me that she was gathering seaweed at the other end of the shore when you were sunbathing—and she always carries a big wicker basket—"

I remembered something else. "I was wakened by a loud noise. Something scared the seagulls and sent them screeching into the sky. I thought it might be someone out shooting rabbits."

We exchanged wild glances.

"That basket she carries, Danny. She could have concealed a gun."

"And that was why you didn't find a weapon beside him," Danny added grimly.

"And if she murdered him, then she must have been hiding, watching me all the time, and—"

"And when you went for Dr. Brackley, she took the chance and dragged his body into one of those caves. It wouldn't have been too difficult. Bodies can be dragged along sand quite easily, I'm sure. And the caves and crevasses aren't too distant. She could be pretty certain that by the time you got back, the tide would be in anyway."

He looked at me triumphantly. "Stands to reason, if she's lived here so long and goes to the shore nearly every day, then she knows all about the caves and tides too."

He paused. "I've just had another idea, Annie. Something we haven't considered so far. Where did she get all the money needed to start that factory? A lot of money—I bet that hasn't occurred to anyone."

"You think she might have found the stolen hoard?"

"Don't you? And somehow, by what means we don't know exactly yet, this Italian guy found out. Who knows? He might have been tracking her down for years. He comes and finds her—perhaps blackmail was involved and she wouldn't play ball."

Danny's explanation was the perfect answer to the mystery of the killer's identity. I wondered why on earth I hadn't thought of it myself. It was so simple.

Almost too simple as it turned out.

CHAPTER 17

The more I thought about it, the more strongly I felt that Mrs. Laverock, who was a woman of mystery, was prime suspect in the murder of Danny's look-alike. And the more certain I became that Danny and I had hit on the truth: that the stolen hoard the Italian prisoners of war had hidden more than fifty years ago was the reason behind it all.

There was only one thing that baffled me. I still didn't know why Mrs. Laverock had tried to kill me on the cliff path, but I was determined to solve both crimes before I left Stormer.

My main mission to solve the mystery surrounding my mother's life was over. She had drowned with her lover, and I had come to terms with my father's refusal to talk about her. I did not doubt that his motives were in my best interests. She was dead and he wished to spare me the details of how she had died, abandoning us both.

My quest had not been in vain. I had gathered one piece of vital information—that I was not responsible for that last vital drama in her life.

All the blame lay with Jetta MacVae, who had rushed out with a rifle to kill them both. One bullet had hit the boat and while reloading, the trigger had gone off and hit her leg, laming her for life. Meanwhile the boat sank, taking the escaping lovers to their deaths.

But I had been beside her and I had seen my mother drown before my eyes. I had been so terrified of the shooting, the madwoman at my side, bleeding, holding the rifle, that I had run away. When they found me—I presume it was my father who led the rescuers—I had blacked out the tragic incident from my memory. All that remained was a nightmare from which there was no escape—that I was in some way responsible for her death.

It was partly Dad's fault, Danny told me when I discussed it with him after we made our discovery about Mrs. Laverock. "If he had told you the truth right at the beginning, as soon as you were old enough to understand, you would never have had these nightmares or the terrible guilt complex."

Danny was right, of course.

Then he looked at his watch and said he must go back to the hotel. He hadn't intended staying away so long. He'd only come to leave a message for me about having our evening meal at the hotel.

"What shall we do about Mrs. Laverock?" I asked.

He frowned. "Do, Annie? Nothing, of course. What can we do?"

"I don't feel like letting her get away with murder without making some kind of effort," I said indignantly.

Danny shook his head. "All right. We both think she

killed the poor Italian guy because she thought he was on to the truth."

"Another thing has just occurred to me, Danny," I interrupted. "I'll bet that she even tried to put him on a false scent when she saw how alike you were. Perhaps she told him a lie, said that you were related to the Italians, that it was you he was looking for."

Danny smiled broadly. "Well done, Annie. That's absolutely brilliant. You know, I'm beginning to think you might have an end to all this mystery. But sadly, it doesn't get us very much further, does it? What did you have in mind—that we confront Mrs. Laverock? That might be dangerous."

"We could tell the police."

"Wait a minute, Annie. You know we can't do that. We don't have a body to produce—they'll never believe us. Where's the evidence?"

I thought of my drawing in lipstick on a sheet of the local newspaper. Somehow I didn't think that would be taken very seriously as evidence.

I said, "Let's not forget she also tried to kill me,"

Danny frowned. "When was that, Annie?"

"On the cliff path—remember? The first day I arrived when I'd been to collect Mrs. MacVae's pills from Dr. Brackley."

Danny shook his head. "I'm still not convinced about that."

"Oh, so you still believe it was a sheep grazing on the cliff top that dislodged the rock. Even after all we've worked out pointing to Mrs. Laverock, who was walking on the path just a few yards in front of me—and who conveniently disappeared just before the rock hurtled down," I said angrily.

Danny sighed. "We've been over all this, Annie. We think that she killed the Italian guy, but why on earth should she want to kill you? There has to be a motive—unless she's a homicidal maniac."

That was true. Even though I suspected Mrs. Laverock, there wasn't any reason for murdering me.

"She nearly died of fright when I told her I was called Bridie Ann."

Danny laughed. "Maybe the name has bad vibes for her."

"Like it had for Jetta MacVae? But she had more reason to hate me, since my mother went off with her husband."

As I was telling Danny, I realized that I had hit on the truth.

"Of course! I've got it—the reason why I was attacked. It was raining and I was carrying Jetta's umbrella. Mrs. Laverock couldn't see my face, so she thought I was Jetta!"

"Good Lord—you may be right." Then Danny looked doubtful. "Jetta has quite a lot of enemies, I should think. She doesn't exactly endear herself to anyone, I gather from Martha. She's a bitter, angry woman, but why should Mrs. Laverock want to kill her as well as the Italian? It just doesn't make sense."

And of course, he was right. It didn't make sense.

After Danny left, I thought it all out from the very beginning. Everything that had happened, episode by episode. And it was then I saw all the flaws in this argument. It just didn't hang together.

It was very unlikely that Mrs. Laverock had some deep-seated reason for hating Jetta. She kept to herself and, apart from buying her groceries, didn't mix with the village folk.

If the Italians' stolen hoard was involved, then Jetta couldn't have any connection. I knew from Martha that Jetta had been merely a child at the time. And at a rough guess, so was Mrs. Laverock fifty years ago. But in her case, since so little was known about her, there might be a family connection that had brought her to Stormer in the first place.

My thoughts turned to Jetta, searching for a motive and an opportunity. I remembered when I returned to the manse her mother said that she had been gone since early morning and had left her without any pills. Jetta came in when I got back from Dr. Brackley and said the pills were there all the time. The sinister conclusion was that I had been deliberately sent out to collect more.

In other words I had been set up. Jetta knew how dangerous the cliff path was and she had guessed at our first meeting that I was Bridie Ann's daughter. She had never ceased to hate the woman through the years. She blamed Bridie not only for taking her husband but for the lameness that had blighted her life. Did her tortured reasoning see the killing of Bridie's daughter as the ultimate revenge?

In other words, were there two different crimes, unrelated to one another? Jetta's revenge on Bridie Ann and Mrs. Laverock's murder of the young Italian?

I went across to the kitchen. Martha was sitting by the window reading a paperback. She put it down as I came in, smiled, and said, "Can I get you anything, my dear?"

I said no, now that the rain had stopped I thought I would take a stroll along the shore. As she put out a hand for her book balanced on the arm of her chair, it slipped onto the floor. I knelt down to pick it up for her and saw that it was Umberto Eco's *Name of the Rose* in the original Italian.

When I said how much I admired a reader tackling a book I had found difficult enough in the English translation, she smiled. "Thank you, my dear," She tapped the book with a finger: "I was always good at languages and I used to enjoy reading books as their authors had written them. But I must confess I find it difficult these days. One needs to keep in constant practice."

She looked at the book critically and said, "Danny lent me this one. He's good at languages too—should have been a scholar, you know. He has a fine mind, quite wasted as a chef."

As I walked toward the shore, I thought of Danny's books in the van. Martha was right. I felt there was a lot more to him than I would ever have the chance to discover before our ways parted forever.

The tide was still well out and I think even before I left the manse I knew what I intended to do. I was going to explore those caves. If the Italian's body had not been washed away, it might still be there with some shred of evidence to link Mrs. Laverock with the murder.

At that moment, I thought I heard my name. I turned and saw her. She was still a far distance away along the beach, but she was beckoning to me.

There was no one in sight. She had guessed that I'd found her out, I thought, and I'm ashamed to say that I panicked and completely lost my nerve.

I was in very great danger. I must escape, not by the cliff path since to reach it I would have to go back toward her. She was carrying the large basket for her seaweed which doubtless contained the weapon she had used to kill the Italian and would use again on me!

I looked around. Any attempt to climb the sheer rock face of the cliff would be madness. Even if I were skilled enough to get a foothold, she could easily pick me off at first shot. The cliffs or the cave? I had little option. Face her and be killed or run for dear life!

I sprinted across, leaping over rocks until at last I was

hidden from the shore. To my left the cliff face was eroded at the base. It looked as if there might be caves in which I could hide until I thought of some way of giving her the slip.

At last I found myself in a wide cavern, very gloomy and smelling strongly of dead fish. Even as I settled down behind a large rock, I saw the footprints I had left and my heart sank.

Of course, I hadn't taken into account the vital fact that she knew the cliffs better than I did and too late I remembered Danny's warning.

I heard her breathing nearby. "Annie? Annie?"

I was lost. Of course it had been easy for her to follow me. I stayed silent, and then I saw her outlined against the mouth of the cave. "Annie? Where are you? I want to talk to you." She was walking toward me. "Why are you hiding? I have something very important to tell you."

She was at the rock, looking over, smiling down at me. "Annie, whatever are you doing, running away from me? Come out."

I came out; there was nothing else I could do. She stretched out her hand and touched my arm.

"Leave me alone! Leave me alone!" I pushed her aside, but her grip was firm.

"What on earth is the matter? I'm not trying to harm you!"

"Did you say that to the Italian fellow you shot yesterday?"

"I—what? What on earth are you talking about?"

I realized I had been mad to let her know. What had made me accuse her, here in this gloomy cavern, when in all probability she had a gun hidden under the seaweed?

"I found him dead. I found his body and when I went

to get Dr. Brackley, it disappeared."

She shook her head. She certainly was a good actress to look so bewildered. "I honestly don't know what you're talking about. I met a foreign lad in the village and he was looking for Danny Lucas. I didn't know he had been killed—this is terrible. Are you sure?"

She looked at my face. "Of course you are. I know that expression—I've seen it so many times in dreams through the years," she added sadly. "When you were a little girl, you often looked like that. I had forgotten."

I stared at her. "Since you know so much about me, perhaps you'll tell my why you tried to kill me on the cliff path the other day. Come on, I want to know."

She shook her head. "Annie, why should I want to kill you?" And taking my arm gently she whispered, "Annie, don't you know?"

I just stared at her as she dragged off the sun hat and dark glasses.

"I'm your mother. All these years and I thought you were lost forever, that I'd never see you again. My punishment for abandoning you, your father said. And then when you walked into the factory, when you said your name, I knew my little girl had come back into my life again."

She shivered. "Let's get out of here and I'll tell you all about it. It's dangerous—we might be caught by the tide."

As we went toward the door, we heard another voice. "Worse than that, you might be caught by me."

A figure stood against the light at the entrance to the cave. The sunlight glinted on a rifle. There was no escape. "A touching scene, one well worth waiting for. The mother and daughter reunited—in death."

My mother cried out and thrust me behind her as the shots echoed around the cave.

CHAPTER 18

Calum's Story

Annie Kelty was the most beautiful girl in the world for me. She'd been everything I've ever wanted from the first day I saw her. As a cop on the beat, I used to walk past her father's bookshop on the Royal Mile in Edinburgh. I could hardly believe my good fortune when I knew that the feeling was mutual and she agreed to marry me.

But when? It was always next month, next summer, next winter—perhaps. And that was how all the trouble started between us. Once I got my promotion to detective sergeant I had everything to offer her—or so I thought. Money to buy a house, start a family. Why wait?

But that wasn't enough for Annie. She wanted adventure, excitement—more than being a suburban wife in Edinburgh could provide for her. She'd got the bit between her teeth when her father had been falsely accused of murder. All on her own, she set out to prove his innocence. Her success convinced her that she had the makings of a private eye.

Gee! How little she knew about the business. However, the next thing she did was get involved in mayhem and murder in a Highland castle, delivering a precious goblet to one of Hamish's customers. Once again, she managed to bring the villains to justice.

I was beginning to feel that I'd never persuade her to give it all up for the normal home life of a policeman's wife. Then we went to Airdbenn for the wedding. She loved it. She was so happy and loving, sighing over the happy couple, so I thought, "This is it. Get the wedding day fixed—now. Once we get to Oban and she sees our Belfast cousins, Maeve and Gerry and their lovely kids— she always goes a bit broody over wee babies—so if that doesn't do the trick, I'll get Mum to work on her too."

And what happened? Like an idiot I didn't suspect that Jim's whiskey especially reserved for Highland weddings was being dished out in lethal doses.

It was like I had been kicked in the head—and the gut—by a runaway horse. Well, what happened after that was that my Annie decided she'd been let down and that instead of waiting until I recovered, she'd go to Stormer and get that knitting yarn for Susie.

These good works, of course, were a coverup to disguise the fact that when she was in the Highlands, she had heard that Stormer might be a link with the mystery of her mother's disappearance. Hamish Kelty had told everyone that she was dead, and long ago Annie had got some queer idea that she had been responsible for her mother's death.

She'd been having nightmares. I wanted her to see a good analyst to sort out those guilt feelings, but Annie had never thought of that. Her mission in life was to find out what had really happened the day her mother departed from her life forever. Hamish, of course, hadn't helped much by refusing to discuss the matter with her.

Hamish is that kind of man who is shy about emotions and plays his cards close to his chest. I guess he had his reasons, but it would have been more sensible if he'd sat down and told Annie the whole truth once she was a big girl and old enough to take it.

"I can't marry you until I know what happened. What if the truth is that I killed my own mother?" Annie demanded when I suggested this to her. "How would you feel about having a murderess as a wife?"

Well, to be honest, I loved her so much I could have lived with that. I could have forgiven and forgotten anything she had done as a tiny, terrified child. . . . But to return to Airdbenn and that wedding. When I surfaced again, I found Annie had gone to Stormer alone. I was pretty annoyed, to put it mildly, and for once I wasn't going to throw everything down and charge after her like a knight on a white horse.

Let her work it out her own way. She couldn't come to much harm, though I doubted whether she'd find out the truth. Perhaps if she didn't this time, after all her efforts, she'd let it all go and get on with her own life. She'd settle down as a wife and in due course, as we both hoped, have kids.

So I went to Oban to meet the Irish cousins. They were a terrific pair and their four kids were cute. Mum was having the time of their life, renewing old acquaintances, having the whole Belfast clan around her.

As for me, I was enjoying every minute, knowing Annie would be with me in a day or two. Then I got that call from her, saying that she wasn't coming on the bus and Danny the fiddler was bringing her to Oban.

It so happened that I remembered Danny very well. He had the kind of John Travolta looks that women go wild about and that put the men in their lives on guard. I also remembered how he had eyed her as we danced past the band during the *ceilidh* and how she had pretended not to notice, but she couldn't fool me.

And then when I had to leave suddenly to throw up, Jim told me that the fiddler had leaped down from the band and come right across to her. Jim, being a good buddy, had cut in and had been given some black looks from Danny.

And now what do I hear? That he's in Stormer and has been with her since she left the wedding and me in my sickbed. Gee, I felt sicker than ever. It's difficult as the coins in a telephone meter keep reminding you that your time is running out, and there's no chance of putting forward a good argument or any argument at all.

But I had made plans with the Belfast family and I didn't want to let them down, so I resigned myself to having to wait and fume until she arrived on the doorstep with the fiddler. I consoled myself that as she was boarding at the manse, she couldn't come to much harm. Which just proved what a fool I was!

However, the way things turned out, when Sean and I were on the golf course with Gerry, I was hailed by an old buddy. We'd both been cops on the beat in our early days with the Edinburgh police, but Jock had got a transfer, married a Highland girl, and landed up in Oban. It was great seeing him again. We went for a drink in the clubhouse and he brought me right up to date.

"Married yet?" he asked.

"Not yet. Soon maybe."

He grinned. "Congratulations! Never thought of you as the marrying kind, you lucky devil."

Hastily, I told him about Annie.

"So where is she?"

"Visiting a place called Stormer—don't suppose you've ever heard of it?"

"Stormer! Do I know it? God, yes, the back of beyond. They haven't set foot in the twentieth century yet. There's absolutely nothing there but wild seas, seals, and nutcases."

"Nutcases?" I asked.

"Sure. There was an attempt by grave robbers a few months ago. I thought that sort of crime went out with the Victorians when the medical students couldn't get fresh corpses." He sighed. "There are plenty of corpses these days, more accident cases than we would ever wish to know about."

"So what was in it for them?"

"A piece of old Stormer history as it happened. These guys weren't after fresh meat—they were after lost treasure. Loot hidden by some Italian prisoners during the Second World War, according to the local folk."

"And did you get someone for it?"

"Not a chance. But we did get a very interesting suspect who had been on our books before for another crime." He paused to introduce me to the club captain who was walking past our table with some of his buddies.

When they left he said, "Where was I? Oh yeah, Stormer. Well, Stormer is certainly putting itself on the map these days. Here's another coincidence for you, Calum."

He laughed. "D'you know, nobody had ever heard of Stormer in years and now I've heard about it twice within the last twelve hours. I was the duty officer last night—you get all sorts of crazy calls—and I had one from a nutcase in Stormer, saying he was a doctor and that a young lass, a visitor, had seen a dead man on the shore that afternoon. He said she had come to him in a panic saying this guy had been shot through the head. When I asked him for more details, this doctor fellow said he had gone back with her, but unfortunately the body had disappeared. Disappeared! Nutcases! What will they think of next?"

As I listened to Jock, I had gone quite cold. Annie had mentioned finding a dead man just before the coins ran out.

And knowing Annie, I knew that was one damn good reason why she wanted to stay in Stormer. Whether she fancied the fiddler or not, I could read her like a book, and I knew that somehow she had got herself involved in another murder case. And I also knew for sure that if I didn't do something about it, one of these days she'd run out of luck and find herself the murder victim!

So I said to Jock, "I think you'd better take that phone call seriously." He looked at me as if I'd taken leave of my senses. "You see, this girl the old man mentioned happens to be my Annie."

I told him about her call from Stormer. "She'd never imagine a dead man lying on the shore at Stormer. She fancies herself as a private eye or an amateur detective—in fact, she's been pretty good at it although I hate to admit it. She's a natural at crime-solving and in the last year she's been directly responsible for bringing killers to justice."

And I quickly outlined the two cases that Annie had been involved in.

At the end of it Jock said, "Maybe we'd better get her onto that other crime I was telling you about. We have a suspect, an unsolved murder." As I listened I felt myself going even colder with horror.

"I think Annie will lead us to this suspect as well." I stood up. "I'm going to Stormer right now. Just pray I'm still in time."

Jock was impressed and he nodded. "I'll come with you, Calum. And take a back-up team and a sniffer dog—he'll find that body wherever it's hidden if the sea hasn't washed it away."

I hardly dared breathe all the way to Stormer. If there'd been time I'd have had Mum light a candle for Annie and say a novena. The distance wasn't far. In normal times I'd hardly have noticed it, but that day it seemed like the end of God's earth, and thirty minutes felt like a hundred years.

Our first stop was to ask for the manse. This old lady, Mrs. MacVae, greeted us by saying that Annie had gone out for a walk along the shore. "About half an hour ago. You've just missed her, but she should be back shortly."

We raced down to the shore, but it was deserted. The tide moving in fast told us we hadn't too much time to lose in finding her. But we hadn't a clue where to look. I dashed back into the MacVaes' house and said, "I'm Annie's boyfriend. We think she might be in danger—caught by the tide. May I see her room please?"

She grumbled a bit about that, but the uniformed policemen on her front doorstep convinced her that we were here in good faith and that she wasn't going to be mugged. She pointed up in the right direction, asking what had the young lady done?

"We don't usually let out rooms, but she seemed such a nice honest lass. What do you think you're doing—?" she protested as I seized Annie's T-shirt nightie, rushed out, and gave it to Jock. Mrs. MacVae was very indignant.

Ignoring her, I said to Jock, "Let's see how good that dog of yours is."

Blazer, that was his name, took one sniff and with a howl that would have had my old dog Nero drop dead with envy, he set off at a cracking pace. Dragging Jock at the end of his chain, with me and the two other cops trying to keep up, he whirled us across the sand toward the cliff face towering sheer above us.

For a moment he hesitated. Then with another plaintive howl, he headed toward an opening in the rock, a cave. By now there were footprints in the wet sand. Three different sets.

Jock seized Blazer's collar and put a hand to his lips. There were voices. Two women were cowering against a rock. One was my Annie. Their assailant was laughing, raising a rifle ready to fire.

We rushed in, but we were too late to stop the bullets' deadly aim.

End of Calum's Story

CHAPTER 19

So this is death.

This is the end of my quest. The rifle shots echoed around the tiny cavern, their sounds magnified, and with a moan my mother slumped down, taking me with her.

"Danny!" I screamed. "Please don't—please!"

As he raised the rifle again, I still couldn't believe it. This must be another part of my nightmare.

Not Danny—dear, kind, understanding Danny, a man I could love. "No—Danny—no!"

I heard him laugh, and in a blinding flash it all became clear. They say that happens in the moment before death when the whole pageant of one's life passes by in a kind of slow-motion drama.

There was another shot, voices, a dog barking—or was it a seal?—and the world went black.

"Annie!" I opened my eyes. They were lifting my

mother's body gently away from me.

"Calum," I whispered. "Oh, Calum, is she dead?"

I heard her groan. "Thank God, thank God," I said.

Calum carried me out of the cave. There were lots of people around and policemen leading Danny away, handcuffed. He turned once and looked back at me. And I still couldn't believe what had happened and that I was still alive, unhurt.

"It's all right, Annie. You'll live and so will the lady who saved your life—"

"Is she hurt badly?"

"Just a flesh wound in her shoulder. A very brave lady, Annie. How will I ever be able to thank her?"

I managed a weak laugh. "You'll think of something, Calum. She's going to be your mother-in-law."

"My—what?"

"I just found out minutes ago that Mrs. Laverock is my mother!"

The police dog was barking and some of the men were scrambling across the rocks, shouting to one another. They had found the murdered man and a bundle of his clothes.

They were just in time; the tide was coming in fast now. All of Stormer it seemed had turned out to witness this new drama. Dr. Brackley was there attending to my mother, seeing her carried safely to the police helicopter that hovered, ready to lift her to the hospital in Oban.

I ran alongside. She pressed my hand and smiled. I leaned over and kissed her.

"I'll be all right, Annie. I could have walked, you know. I've survived worse things. Come and see me before you leave."

The next time I saw her, she was sitting up in bed with her arm in a sling and demanding to go home. By that time I had heard the story from Calum of the miracle that had brought him to Stormer.

"It was Jock telling me about this hoax call. A man calling himself Dr. Brackley had told them about a young lass finding a dead man who disappeared. That was enough to get me started, but then Jock told me about a man wanted for hotel robberies—a chef. He was also wanted on a murder charge. One of the guests—a woman who woke up and saw him—had foolishly attacked him and he'd strangled her.

"To say that my scalp crawled with horror is to put it mildly. I knew you were in mortal danger—that had happened before—I don't know how—"

There were other pieces of the jigsaw that settled into place. When Danny was arrested, they searched his van and the photographs he had hidden were of gravestones in the Stormer churchyard. The story about his being an orphan was a pack of lies.

I had guessed right. He was the grandson of Mario Milano, the informer who had betrayed Volti and Bacchi and made his way back to Italy after the war. Danny's mother had married a penniless Englishman but his grandfather had boasted about the treasure in Scotland, hidden in a grave and waiting to be collected.

The child of a broken home, a drifter, Danny had the makings of a musician and had played his way across Europe and taken jobs in hotels. But the treasure was never far from his mind, and a few months ago he had made his way to Stormer. But Paulo Volti's grandson was also on the trail armed with the photograph of his grandfather at John Smithson's grave where he believed the treasure was hidden.

All three men had been from the same small fishing port in southern Italy, and the buried treasure had become a legend almost as miraculous as the Holy Grail. So Volti came to Scotland hoping he could make a deal with Milano's grandson. When he saw Danny's face on the TV news wanted for the hotel murder, he knew he had found him and tracked him down to Stormer.

But Danny wasn't prepared to make any deal, blackmail or otherwise. He lured Volti to the beach and shot him. He had to wait until Mrs. Laverock and I both left the scene before dragging the body into one of the caves while I went in search of help.

How easily I had been persuaded that Mrs. Laverock was the murderess.

"Is the treasure still there?" I asked Calum.

"No, it disappeared long ago. The photograph would indicate that it was hidden in the blacksmith's grave which had been dug the day before the Italians' escape attempt. When it was opened a few years later to bury his wife, there was no mention of any treasure being found.

"However, according to Dr. Brackley, their son who ran the local garage and helped the old gravedigger suddenly came into a fortune and departed to a new life in Australia. One might come to some interesting conclusions about that particular piece of good fortune."

"So all these deaths were for nothing," I said.

"There are very rarely winners in ill-gotten gains, Annie," said Calum. "Danny realized that the police were onto him for the hotel-room murder. He was keeping a few steps ahead of the law, hoping to find the treasure. He didn't expect that you would have worked it all out. When you did, he knew that you'd have to be silenced too. He didn't bargain for Mrs. Laverock following you and overhearing that she was your mother."

"I was such a fool," I said. "I trusted Danny, believed him—he seemed so, oh well, so nice."

Calum kissed me. He understood a lot more than I gave him credit for.

But the time had come for me to talk to my mother, who was getting stronger every day and ready to leave the hospital. She took me in her arms and I thought how long I had dreamed of a moment like this and never believed it could ever come to pass.

"I suppose you would like to hear what happened that day long ago," she said sadly. "Jetta's shots went wide but hit the boat and sank it. Tom and I managed to swim to one of the islands. I have to be honest with you, darling girl. I should never have married your father—Hamish was in love with me, but marriage was a mistake. I thought I had lost Tom when Jetta said they'd had an affair and there was to be a baby. So I took your father on the rebound.

"I knew when I went back to Stormer that Tom was terminally ill. I doubt if even Jetta knew, but after old Tam's funeral, I knew I would never see Tom again. So we took what fate had given us, the chance of a few months together. I would have forgiven Tom anything and I thought Hamish would forgive me. I thought that was what perfect love was about—total forgiveness—and that I could come back to you both, that he would welcome me back as I had taken Tom back after Jetta."

She sighed. "Hamish was always so mild and unemotional. I expected too much of him and I lost him, but most of all I lost you, my only beloved child. When Tom died, as far as Hamish was concerned, I was dead too. He said he never wanted to set eyes on me again. He was remarrying and his new wife would be a perfect mother to you, Annie.

"That seemed pretty final. So what could I do? I could have fought for you, but I had absolutely nothing to offer and no court would have given custody of the child to the runaway wife who pretended to be dead."

She paused. "Did he ever marry again?"

"Not then, but he has someone now. Someone I like very much."

"I'm glad. He deserves happiness. I let him divorce me on grounds of desertion. Then I was free to come back to Stormer where I had once been so happy. But I was afraid of Jetta, of what she might do if she knew I was still alive.

"So I moved to one of the other islands and started up a weaving group with some other women. It took years and years to build a business, but we were lucky. Some of our knitwear was taken by a London designer. Next it was being bought in America. And five years ago, we bought the old barracks and Laverock Knitwear was born.

"I still didn't want Jetta to find out. I used to see her limping about the village sometimes. Since I had to avoid the sunshine for my skin condition, the sun hat and sunglasses were a great disguise."

She stopped and took my hand. "Darling Annie, can you ever forgive me for deserting you? I've loved you so much through the years, always hoped you were happy. I've even carried your photograph with me." From her handbag she took the photo of a four-year-old. I knew it well. Dad had one just like it.

I kissed her and asked, "What happens now? Do you want Dad to know that I've found you?"

She shrugged. "That's up to you, dear. You know him better than I ever did." She smiled. "You'll be happy with your Calum, a fine lad. I'd love to come to your wedding—"

"That would be wonderful!"

"But I think a little too embarrassing—think of all the explanations!" she said sadly. "Best to keep our discovery a secret—I'd rather Jetta didn't know who I am."

I wondered about Jetta and the false errand I had been sent on that morning when I had narrowly escaped death on the cliff path. She now seemed the prime suspect, but Calum said it was much more likely to have been an accidental rockfall, so I didn't interrupt my mother's story with my suspicions.

"Besides," she said, "I have a life in Stormer—a good life—and as long as we can meet sometimes, then I'm content."

Perhaps she was right. I couldn't honestly see her happy through the years as the wife of an Edinburgh bookseller she didn't love.

Pausing, she hugged me. "Perhaps I'll have grandchildren to look forward to someday, and you'll bring them to see me. God has been good to let me find you again. I can't complain. I've been very lucky."

I wasn't so sure about that, but I knew one thing for certain: that I loved Calum and wanted to marry him more than ever. I'd try to be a good wife even if life wasn't madly exciting. Perhaps he'd let me help him solve a crime now and then.

Life, the great adventure, has just begun. . . .